Listen to the mustn'ts, child,
Listen to the don'ts
Listen to the shouldn'ts
The impossibles, the won'ts
Listen to the never haves
Then listen close to me —
Anything can happen, child,
Anything can be.

—Shel Silverstein

Possibles

VAUNDA MICHEAUX NELSON

The Putnam & Grosset Group

A PaperStar Book, published in 1997 by The Putnam & Grosset Group,
200 Madison Avenue, New York, NY 10016. PaperStar Books
and the PaperStar logo are trademarks of The Putnam Berkley Group, Inc.
Originally published in 1995 by G. P. Putnam's Sons.
Published simultaneously in Canada.
Printed in the United States of America.

Nelson, Vaunda Micheaux. Possibles / Vaunda Micheaux Nelson.
p. cm. Summary: Following the death of her father, a twelve-year-old girl
takes a summer job instead of going to camp with a friend as planned.
[1. Death—Fiction. 2. Grief—Fiction. 3. Afro-Americans—Fiction.] I. Title.
PZ7.N43773Po 1995 [Fic]—dc20 94-44386 CIP AC
ISBN 0-698-11551-1
1 3 5 7 9 10 8 6 4 2

Lines on pages 159 and 160 from "Leaning on the Everlasting Arms,"
copyright © 1887 by Rev. E. A. Hoffman.
"Listen to the Mustn'ts" from *Where the Sidewalk Ends* by Shel Silverstein.
Copyright © 1974 by Evil Eye Music, Inc. Selection reprinted
by permission of HarperCollins Publishers.
Lines on page 7 from "Mother to Son" from *Selected Poems* by Langston Hughes.
Copyright 1926 by Alfred A. Knopf, Inc., and renewed 1954 by Langston Hughes.
Reprinted by permission of the publisher.
Words by Heart by Ouida Sebestyen is published by Little, Brown and Company.

SCRABBLE® is a registered trademark of Hasbro, Inc. © 1982.
Milton Bradley Company is a division of Hasbro, Inc.
All rights reserved. Used with permission.

This is a work of fiction. The events and characters portrayed are imaginary.
Their resemblance, if any, to real-life counterparts is entirely coincidental.

For Drew
with all my heart

Possibles

Chapter 1

"Mary Sheppard Lee."

Sheppy stood up and walked toward the stage to receive her diploma. Mary Sheppard. It had been her grandmother's name, and Sheppy was proud to have it. She had gotten used to kids at Sunday school laughing at Christmas pageant time and whispering, "Sheppard should play a shepherd." Then one year Mr. Batch heard them and said, "Maybe *Mary* would like to play Mary." And Sheppy did. She had even gotten used to kids at school saying, "Hey, Sheppard, where's your sheep?" And she had told Parker Ford that if he called her "German shepherd" one more time, she might show him just how tough a Sheppard could be. She *was* proud of her name. But it didn't really matter anymore because, sometime in the fifth grade, the joking had stopped. She was just Sheppy now.

At the podium, Mrs. Carlson gave Sheppy a large envelope.

"Congratulations," the principal said aloud, shaking her hand. Then she gently squeezed Sheppy's arm and whispered, "Your father would be proud."

Sheppy felt her eyes fill up. *Darn it. Here it comes.* It had been almost two weeks since the funeral. She had come back to school a week ago determined to be strong. Determined not to cry. Why did Mrs. Carlson have to say that?

Back at her seat, Sheppy tried to hold in the tears she felt coming. She looked around the small auditorium. Lots of kids were crying. She glanced over at Tessa. Her friend's cheeks were wet. Even Parker looked sad. They all were leaving Lincoln Elementary. After seven years. Sheppy was, too. She relaxed and let her tears come. It felt good.

"You're gonna be great in junior high," her brother Ranger said at the reception. He hugged her hard, lifting her feet off the cafeteria floor.

"Weren't you just in kindergarten last year?" Mama asked. She touched Sheppy's cheek and smiled. A tired smile.

Sheppy stood sandwiched between Mama and Ranger. She felt safe. Like a caterpillar in a cocoon. Someone took their picture. Sheppy imagined what it would look like. Perfect. Except for one thing. Papa.

"Hey, Shep!"

Sheppy watched Tess pushing her way through the crowd of kids and grown-ups.

"Have some punch and cookies," Sheppy told Mama and Ranger. "I'll be back."

She met Tessa halfway. More hugs.

"Well, we made it," Tess said. "Isn't it great?"

"In a way," Sheppy said. "But now it'll be like starting all over."

"I know what you mean."

Sheppy wasn't sure she did. They hadn't been on quite the same beat lately.

"You just have to promise to keep helping me with English," Tess went on.

"If you promise to keep helping me with math."

"Deal," they said together with a double low five.

"Hey, Germ!"

Sheppy didn't have to turn around to know it was Parker. "Germ" was short for German shepherd. He hadn't said it in over a year. It was strange that his saying it now didn't bother her a bit. Strange that suddenly she kind of liked it, that she felt sorry he was moving away.

"So, Ford, where're you going to be parking yourself next year?" Sheppy said, turning to face him.

He grinned. "Not bad, Sheppard. I guess there's hope for you after all."

Sheppy felt herself blush. She usually wasn't very good at jokes. Wasn't quick enough. Always thought of what she could have said after the moment was over.

"Parker Ford! Was that a compliment? I guess there's hope for you, too," Tess said.

"Never!"

They all laughed.

"So, where *are* you moving?" Tess asked.

"Some dinky little town in West Virginia. My aunt and uncle live down there. We're going to stay with them until we can get our own place," he said, looking away. "Dad got a job in the mines."

Parker wasn't happy about leaving. Sheppy hadn't realized.

"West Virginia's not too far," she said. "Maybe you'll get to come back to visit."

"Maybe."

"It's kind of scary." Tess looked at Sheppy. "How everything's changing."

"Nothing to be scared of," Parker said. He smiled and winked at Sheppy. "Except maybe Germs."

Sheppy pretended to look mad.

"Where's your mom today, Parker?" Tess asked. "I didn't see her in the auditorium."

"She couldn't come," he said, his eyes shifting to the floor.

Something was wrong. Sheppy wanted to ask, but could tell Parker was uncomfortable.

Without deciding to, she touched his arm. "I'll miss you, Park," she caught herself saying. He seemed surprised at first, then smiled and lightly punched her shoulder. Sheppy remembered when she didn't even want him for a partner in line. Now she felt like hugging him. Everything *was* changing.

As Parker walked away, Tess said, "Hey, Shep, I have to go, too. My parents are waiting." She squeezed Sheppy's hand. "We're in seventh grade now!"

"Yeah," Sheppy said smiling. "See you." She watched Tess leaving for a moment, then turned to see Parker look back and wave at her before disappearing into the crowd.

Why hadn't Mrs. Ford come to Parker's graduation? Nothing would have kept Papa from coming today. Nothing. Papa would have been there. He would have been there when she graduated from high school and college, too. When she did anything important in her life, he would have been there. If it were possible. But it wasn't. Not anymore.

Chapter

2

Listen to the mustn'ts, child,
Listen to the don'ts
Listen to the shouldn'ts
The impossibles, the won'ts
Listen to the never haves
Then listen close to me—
Anything can happen, child,
Anything can be.

They were the last words she'd spoken to Papa. A Shel Silverstein poem. She had first read it to him when he was in the hospital. When there was still hope.

"Let me see," he said. His eyes looked tired, but he was smiling. He read it out loud three times. Papa was a great reader, a great storyteller.

Sheppy remembered Ranger's sixteenth birthday. Everybody was talking at once when Papa started to recite "Mother to Son" by Langston Hughes. He didn't make an announcement or shout or anything. He had just been talking with Ranger and started to speak the lines. He'd changed it a little. Instead of beginning, "Well, son," he'd said, "Well, Range, I'll tell you: Life for me ain't been no crystal stair . . ." His deep, baritone voice filtered through the room, beckoning. And by the time he had finished, people were gathered around and nobody was anywhere but with Papa. And Langston Hughes.

One day after Papa had come home from the hospital, Sheppy'd heard him reciting the Silverstein lines quietly to himself. And she had whispered them to him before going to bed on that last night. Like Papa, she had changed the poem a little. She'd said, "Listen to the mustn'ts, Papa."

The doctors had been full of impossibles and won'ts. It was why they'd let him come home. But Papa had made her a believer, told her never to give up on anything, so she prayed for a miracle, a *possible*. Prayed that his sunken cheeks would suddenly fill out. That his thin, bony arms would be strong again with the muscles that had swung her, lifted her, hugged her all her life. Prayed that he would jump right out of bed and shout, "It's gone!" But the cancer hadn't gone. Papa had.

That's the way Mama had said it that morning. "Sheppy, honey, he's gone."

"Who?" Sheppy had said. And she wondered why her mother held her so tight. Sheppy had fallen asleep thinking about the possibles. Believing. So who had gone?

Gone. No one yet had said that her father had died. Was dead. Even the doctor asked, "What time did he *pass*?" And visitors said, "So sorry to hear about *your loss*." "He's with God now." "He's at peace." "His suffering's over."

Sheppy hadn't said it either. Part of her thought that maybe, if nobody said "The End," the story would go on. Papa's story. His life. Maybe if he was only "gone," he could one day come walking through the door. "I'm back!"

Maybe if she was younger, she could have believed that. She'd believed in Santa Claus long after her classmates had stopped. Ranger kept telling her he was real, and she believed everything Ranger said. People were always telling lies to protect other people from something. Always waiting for just the right moment to give bad news. Like the time Mama let her open a birthday present early just before telling her that Tess was too sick to come to her party. Sheppy had hated being the youngest. Being treated like a baby.

Now she *wanted* to be treated like a baby. Felt like one. But Mama had come right out and told her. Sheppy was old enough now. Twelve. Old enough to know that this was really the end of Papa's story. No more adventures.

• • •

"Shep?" Ranger wrapped his arms around her from behind. "Everyone's leaving for graduation parties. Come on. We have something special planned."

"Yes," Mama said, "this is a day to celebrate."

Sheppy turned and buried her face in Ranger's chest.

8

Chapter

3

Two days after graduation, Sheppy found herself in the same navy blue dress she'd worn to the funeral. She hadn't wanted to wear it ever again.

"This is it," Mama said as she turned the car into the driveway of a gray house with white shutters at the windows.

Sheppy felt wet under her arms. Nerves. Her tendency to sweat, *perspire* as Mama always said, embarrassed her. She was glad she'd worn the dress now. The dark circles that often formed on her clothes might not show. "Ready?" Mama asked, turning off the engine.

No, Sheppy wasn't ready. She'd never been on a real job interview before. She'd done a little baby-sitting, but always for friends. People she knew and liked. People who knew and liked her. People who wouldn't care about sweat marks because they knew she showered every day. No, Sheppy wasn't ready.

"I'm ready."

"That's my girl," Mama said. She straightened Sheppy's collar. "Now, remember. Just be yourself. They're going to like you."

A part of Sheppy hoped they wouldn't, but she knew the money was important to her family.

Once outside the car, Sheppy studied the house and yard. The grass looked like a carpet in a room where kids weren't allowed. Flowers were perfectly placed along the sides of the house, around a birdbath, in boxes outside the windows, like in storybook pictures.

At the door, Mama motioned for Sheppy to ring the bell. Mama was letting her know she wasn't going to do this for her, that Sheppy would have to do her own talking.

Sheppy was tall, but the gray-haired man who answered the door made her feel the way a sparrow must feel next to a hawk. She had to bend her neck way back to see his face.

"Mrs. Lee and . . . Mary is it?" Mr. Montgomery said. "Come right in."

"It's Sheppy, sir." Mama had taught her to say "ma'am" and "sir." She smiled hard and shook his outstretched hand. His hand was large, but the handshake was limp and cool.

They entered the house into a hall with doorways leading off on either side and a staircase directly in front of them. They walked through one of the doorways, through the living room, and into the dining room. The inside of the house was neat like the outside, as if nobody lived here. Everything was old. Not worn-out old. Antique.

Mr. Montgomery offered them chairs and then iced tea from a pitcher that matched glasses arranged on a tray.

Sheppy wasn't sure if it was more polite to say, "No, thank you," or if it would be better to take some since he'd already gone to the trouble.

Be yourself, Mama had said. Sheppy was thirsty, so she said, "Thank you very much, sir."

Mama smiled and said, "Yes, thank you."

Sheppy relaxed a little. She'd said the right thing. They sat at the table and Mr. Montgomery took a chair across from them.

"Here's the situation," he said, looking at Mama. "My niece is recovering from an accident. She had a very bad leg break a week ago and, although the bones have been pinned and her leg is in a cast, her physicians have told her not to put weight on it for four to six weeks, and to keep it elevated as much as possible. So I don't want her to be alone here. Our neighbor, Rose Fletcher, will come in the morning and stay until noon, when she goes to visit her mother at a nursing home. She can be back at three. So I need a person to cover those hours. A person who is reliable."

He stared at Sheppy, as if trying to find the word RELI-ABLE written somewhere on her face. She sat up straighter.

"The person would have to serve Constance her lunch," he continued, "although Mrs. Fletcher would have most things prepared ahead of time. There, of course, should be enough for two. The person would clean up after lunch and fill any other requests my niece may have. This would include helping her when she needs to use the bathroom. So it must be someone who isn't squeamish about such things. Constance prefers being taken to the bathroom across the hall, but we've put a portable toilet chair in her room, as well as a bedpan. She may want someone to talk to, so the person should not be timid. I want someone who is attentive, but who also will know when to give my niece time to rest."

The person. The someone. Would it be Sheppy? Mr. Montgomery seemed to be talking exclusively to Mama, but Sheppy thought she should ask a question. Maybe it would make her seem not too timid.

"When would I . . . *the person* start?"

"A week from tomorrow," he said, finally looking right at Sheppy. "I've taken some time off from work until then." He stared at Sheppy a moment, then turned back to Mama and said, "Frankly, I was interested in someone older than your daughter, a college student perhaps. But Harvey Davis has explained your circumstances and has very good things to say about your family. Davis is a good man. I trust him. And it could be that Constance would enjoy having a younger person around. She's twenty-six but has been out in the world very little."

Mama nodded.

"Now Mary," he said, shifting in his seat. "I have a few questions for you."

Sheppy shifted, too. Her palms were sweaty.

"Are you comfortable using kitchen appliances such as a stove?"

"Yes, sir. I sometimes help fix meals at home."

"What would you do if something went wrong here?"

"I guess I'd call you, or 911 if it was an emergency."

"What might you do to help my niece pass the time?"

Sheppy thought a moment. "I'd try to find out what she wanted to do. Play cards maybe or a board game if she likes that." She thought of Papa lying in his bed. He loved a good game of 500 rummy or Monopoly. But most of all . . . "I might read to him," she said in a whisper.

She felt suspended, caught in a single frame of a movie.

"Excuse me?" Mr. Montgomery's voice brought her back.

Sheppy's eyes came to focus on a vase of daisies across the room. Quickly she shifted her gaze back to Mr. Montgomery and said, "I might read to Miss Montgomery, sir, and maybe play music on the radio or stereo if you have one. The kind of music she likes."

He sat looking at her for a moment. His face didn't show whether he liked what Sheppy said or not. He stood up, poured everyone more tea, and went to stand in front of the window, looking out. With his back to them he said, "I'll pay fifteen dollars a day for the three hours."

Wow! She did some quick math in her head. Seventy-five dollars a week. Mama said Mr. Montgomery would probably pay well, but Sheppy hadn't expected this. She tried not to let her surprise show.

"But I won't make a final decision until Constance has

had a chance to meet the girl," Mr. Montgomery said, turning again to Mama. "I'll go and see if she's ready."

He put down his glass, went through the hallway and up the stairs.

Mama squeezed Sheppy's hand as if to say, "You're doing fine." Sheppy smiled slightly and relaxed. She straightened the skirt of her dress and made sure her knees were together with her feet crossed at the ankles, like Mama had taught her.

Sheppy could hear Mr. Montgomery saying something. The voice was coming through a small wooden door between the kitchen and the dining room. She was studying the door, wondering, when Mama whispered, "Probably a laundry chute." A laundry chute. Sheppy had seen them in movies, and usually something funny ended up falling through. But she didn't laugh at what came down next. It was a woman's voice, loud and tight, saying, "Does it matter what I think?"

Silence. Sheppy felt a drop of sweat run slowly down her side. Mr. Montgomery spoke again, quietly, then Sheppy heard him coming back down the stairs.

"It seems Constance isn't feeling up to visitors today," he said, stopping to stand behind the chair he had been sitting in. His eyebrow twitched. "But we've discussed the matter, and if your daughter wants the job, Mrs. Lee, she's hired."

Mama looked at her and said, "Sheppy?"

Three hours a day with that cranky woman? No, ma'am.

Sheppy didn't want the job. "I'll take the job, Mr. Montgomery," she said. "Thank you."

"Thank *you*," he said, shaking her hand. "My niece may seem a bit particular about some things. But I'm sure once you two get to know each other, you'll get along fine." He walked them to the door. "We'll expect you Monday after next at noon then. Oh, and Mary, you may dress casually when you come. I want you to be comfortable, and I wouldn't want you to soil your better clothing in the kitchen."

"Thank you," Mama said, shaking his hand.

After they were outside, Mama gave Sheppy a hug and said, "I'm proud of you, honey."

"Thanks, Mama." Sheppy was glad to have made her happy. But she wasn't so sure about herself. Or Miss Constance Montgomery.

Chapter

4

Tess's old plaid duffel bag lay open on the bed with the usual camp gear surrounding it. Flashlight, soap, toothbrush, toothpaste, towel, washcloth, *Ghost Stories You'll Wish You Never Heard*. Sheppy pushed back and forth in Tessa's rocking chair. How she would miss those stories. Penknife, mess kit, raincoat, boots. One year it rained almost the whole three weeks. She and Tess had complained about being wet and cold. Now, Sheppy would have welcomed three weeks of snow to be able to go to Camp Walking Bear with Tess. Camp Walking *Bare* they called it.

"I thought you were going to kiss Parker Ford at the reception!" Tess said. She hugged a sweatshirt she was folding and kissed the air.

"I didn't kiss him."

"Well, almost." Tess tucked the sweatshirt into her suitcase. "What were you doing?"

Sheppy shrugged. "Parker's okay."

"He's okay if you like lizards."

"Well, maybe I do like lizards," Sheppy said. She and Tess had been friends since first grade, when Tess had moved to town. Sheppy usually didn't mind her teasing, but today she wasn't in the mood.

Tess didn't say anything, just looked away, pretending to be giving attention to her packing. Sheppy was sorry she'd snapped at her. It was quiet except for the soft sound of shirts and socks going into the suitcase, the occasional clink or thump of an alarm clock or a pair of shoes being dropped in.

Tessa finally broke the silence. "Has your mama found a job yet? I mean, besides the Laundromat?"

That's what Tess had been doing lately. Changing the subject. She'd been the one who said, "Let's always talk about everything. Even the bad things." She was the one who would force Sheppy to sit down and speak her mind. "Sit!" she'd say, pointing her finger. "Now, speak!" she'd command.

Sheppy would play along and bark until they were both laughing. Then they'd have a good, serious talk. She wished Tessa would play the dog game now.

"Mama got a job with a housecleaning service. It's only part-time. And Ranger's working for a landscaping company, cutting grass and doing other yard stuff up on Beacon Heights."

"Hey! Those people are pretty rich. Maybe you could still come to camp."

"Tessy, I *told* you. I can't come."

"Well, you don't have to yell at me. I'm getting the feeling that you really don't want to come. I just thought camp might cheer you up after . . ." She didn't finish. Just kept packing.

After what? After the funeral? After your father . . . would she have said, "died"?

Tess was right in a way. Part of Sheppy didn't want to go to camp, the part that was scared. Scared that something might happen to Mama, too. But a big part of her wanted to go more than anything, the part that listened to the possibles. Maybe if she went to camp, things would seem normal again. Maybe she could even pretend none of the past few months had happened, that when she came home Papa would be there as always.

"I didn't mean to yell," Sheppy said. "I'm sorry." She stared at the floor, wishing.

"Didn't your dad have insurance?" Tess asked.

"Yes, but some of it was used for the funeral, and Mama says we have to save the rest for college. Ranger will be going in a year. He wants to get into that big music school, Juilliard. I think he's good enough. And Papa said so."

"I thought he was talking about joining the Air Force?"

"Not anymore," Sheppy said. "Mama told me that Ranger didn't really want to go into the service. He just thought it would be easier on the family because if he went in the Air Force he could go to school later and the government would help pay for it. But Mama said he was talking

18

crazy. She said she wouldn't let Ranger give up his dream."

"My mom says that you can't always have everything the way you want it," Tess said. "She says you have to make sacrifices sometimes." Sheppy imagined Tess saying that to *her* and pointing a huge finger in her face.

"I know," she said. "Mama and Papa always say that kind of stuff, too. But then there was that time Papa went out and bought a second-hand piano when they didn't have much money." Sheppy loved this story. "Remember, I told you."

"Yeah, so?"

"So it was right after they got married. They didn't have any furniture. They were sleeping on a mattress on the floor and Papa came home one day with a piano."

"Why?" Tess stopped packing and frowned. "I guess I never really understood that."

Sheppy was frustrated. She never used to have to explain so much to Tess. They'd always just understood each other, often without talking. Like radar. She looked down at the carpet, at the ink stain left there a year ago when they'd tried using a fountain pen for the first time.

"I guess because sometimes being happy is more important than other things, like furniture."

"Oh," Tess said.

There was silence again. Then the sound of a zipper. Sheppy looked up to see Tess carefully putting her underpants in a red cloth bag. Sheppy had a blue one just like it. Their UP (underpants) Safety Packs. Each bag actually had *two* short zippers that met in the middle and a tiny padlock to keep them together.

She and Tess had invented the idea after being victims of panty raids at camp three years in a row. They were tired of having to pick their underwear off a tree in front of what seemed like the whole world. It would be especially awful this year if their bras were stolen. They'd told Mama what they wanted to do, and she'd made the bags for them. Sheppy wouldn't even have a chance to test hers. At least not this year.

"You'll have to let me know how the Safety Pack works," Sheppy said, breaking the silence. She knew how to change the subject, too.

"Yeah," Tess said without looking at her. More silence. Then the *click* of the lock being snapped shut.

"Tess," Sheppy said, "I do want to go. Honest. We don't have the money. Even with Ranger's job, and Mama's, too. The hospital keeps sending bills and . . . never mind." She focused again on the ink stain.

Tess dropped something on the bed, came over and knelt on the floor in front of her.

"I'm sorry, Shep," she said. "I just want things to be the way they were."

Things can never be the way they were, Sheppy wanted to say. Instead she hugged her friend and said, "Promise you'll write?"

"If you'll promise to write me back. I really want to hear about this lady you have to sit with."

Sheppy suddenly had a thought.

"What I did on my summer vacation," she said, pretending to write in the air. "Lady-sitting."

They laughed, but it felt fake, a bit too loud.

Chapter 5

Sheppy felt a band of heat across her face. Sun. Morning. She had always loved the sheer white curtains that invited sun or moonlight into her bedroom. This morning she pulled the sheet over her head.

"Sheppy?"

She peeked out just enough to see Mama standing in the doorway.

"Don't you think it's about time you got up? It's ten o'clock. There are things to do around here and you have to be at the Montgomerys' by noon."

Sheppy groaned and turned over. She heard Mama coming across the room. Sheppy held the sheet tighter around her and tried to hold in a laugh. She knew what was coming. Mama grabbed the bottom of the sheet and pulled.

"Rise and shine!" Mama sang.

Sheppy squealed as they started a tug-of-war. She pulled with all her strength but knew she could never win. Mama was small, but mighty.

"Okay, okay," Sheppy finally said, letting go of the sheet and sitting up in bed.

"I figured you'd see it my way," Mama said, hands on hips, her thick dark hair mussed in a Hollywood kind of way. Standing there, she looked gorgeous. Still, Sheppy couldn't resist throwing a pillow right in her face.

"Now you've done it," Mama said, coming at her. Sheppy squealed. Mama bopped her on the head with the pillow. Sheppy covered her head with her arms to prepare for another blow. It didn't come. Instead, she felt Mama sit on the bed and pull her into a hug.

"I'm sorry about camp, honey. I know how much you wanted to go."

Sheppy couldn't see her mother's face, but her voice sounded shaky.

"Mama, I . . ." She was going to say "I love you," but the tea kettle made a loud whistle. Mama stood up and started to leave. At the door, she turned with glistening eyes. She paused, then smiled and pointed her finger at Sheppy. "You'd better have your tail out of that bed when I get back."

It was like in those old foreign movies when the actor's lips and the voice that's been dubbed are out of sync. What Mama'd wanted to say in that moment of hesitation was

23

that she missed Papa. Sheppy couldn't have been more sure of that if the words had been written in a balloon over Mama's head, like in a comic strip.

She fell back, hugging her pillow. Bed. She wanted to stay there, stay until someone told her it was safe to come out. But there were chores. And there was Miss Montgomery. It hardly seemed worth missing camp for three measly hours a day. But Mama said the family couldn't make it on just her pay from the Laundromat.

Mama had worked at Harvey's Laundromat for years. When Sheppy was little she'd loved the jangle of all the keys Mama carried for doors and machines. Mama opened the business in the morning, closed it at night, cleaned, collected money from the machines. It was self-service, so she didn't have to be there all day, but she was on call if there were problems. The family's phone number was posted on the wall by the pay phone, so people were always calling about something. Sometimes Mama would just get home from work, the phone would ring, and she'd have to turn around and go right back.

It made Sheppy mad, how strangers kept Mama jumping, like she was a marionette and they were pulling her strings. What made her maddest was that the customers caused most of their own problems. They put too much soap in the washer. They didn't read the signs that said to be careful about putting plastic-lined materials in the dryers. They used a dollar bill that was too worn for the change machine to read.

Once, when Mama was in the back room, Sheppy had

24

taken a Magic Marker and changed the "3" in their phone number to an "8." She figured when customers couldn't reach Mama, they would call the owner, Mr. Davis, instead. His number was written under theirs. Sheppy knew the change would be discovered, but she didn't care. Mama needed a break.

That afternoon Mama came in from planting flowers and said, "Did anybody call?"

"No," Ranger had said. "Some exceptional people must be doing their laundry today."

Mama laughed and said, "Kind of nice, isn't it?" Then she'd picked up the receiver and checked for a dial tone.

No customers called that day. But Mama did get one call just as they were finishing dinner. Mr. Davis. He said a couple of people had phoned him because they couldn't reach her.

He must have asked, "Is everything all right?" because Mama said, "Everything's fine here, but maybe there's something wrong with the line. Sorry about this, Harv."

Sheppy couldn't just sit there while Mama went through the trouble of calling the phone company, so she confessed.

"You what?" Mama exclaimed.

Ranger got up and started the dishes. He wanted to be out of the line of fire.

"I changed the number. I just wanted you to have a day off, that's all."

"You know you caused Mr. Davis a lot of inconvenience. He had to leave his office twice to go up there." Mama was mad.

"But those people cause you inconvenience every day!"

"That's what I get paid for, Sheppy."

"Well, I'm sorry, okay?" Sheppy dropped her fork on her plate, stomped into the living room, and fell into a chair.

Silence.

Then she heard Papa's deep laughter.

"And don't you go making light of this, Norris," Mama said. "This is serious." Her voice was sharp.

Papa cleared his throat and got quiet. After a while, Sheppy peeked around the chair to see Mama sitting hunched over the kitchen table and shaking all over.

Ranger looked up from his dish washing and grinned. Papa started laughing again, too.

"Come here, girl," Mama said. Sheppy ran over and into her open arms. Mama pulled a Kleenex from the box on the table and wiped her eyes, still laughing.

"Don't you ever do anything like this again." She held Sheppy's face in her hands, and kissed both her cheeks. "But thanks."

Sheppy made a new sign and went with Mama to the Laundromat to put it up.

Mama'd told Sheppy that even though there were some frustrations, she did like her job. And she liked Mr. Davis. If the family wanted to go visiting or something, he would take calls that day. They could do their laundry for free. And Mr. Davis had been the one to recommend Sheppy to Mr. Montgomery.

When Mama had said she couldn't go to camp this year,

26

Sheppy had cried, "Aw, Mama, why can't Mr. Davis give you more money? You've worked for him for*ever*. Doesn't he care?"

"Mr. Davis *did* give me a raise," Mama said, "and he *does* care. But he's not a charity. He's doing what he can. And one of the thing's he's done is find you this job. I don't like asking you to give up camp or your summer, but we all need to pitch in here."

Sheppy hated to admit it, but she knew it was fair. Ranger was working. And Mama had taken an extra job. Three hours a day was *more* than fair.

"Sheppy!"

She leaped out of bed and dashed for the bathroom. "I'm up, Mama!"

"Well, hurry down here. Tessa's on the phone."

Chapter

6

"Thank you, honey. We're doing all right," Mama was saying when Sheppy finally got downstairs. "Here's Sheppy now."

"Hey, Tess."

"Hey, Shep. Surprise!"

"Are you calling from camp?"

"Yeah. Mom said I could."

"But you've only been there two days."

Tess giggled. "I know. I couldn't wait."

Sheppy grinned.

"Besides," Tess went on, "I thought today would be good because I know you're starting your lady-sitting job. Are you excited?"

"Thrilled," Sheppy said dramatically. "I just can't wait to help her use the bedpan."

Tess laughed, then said, "Seriously, it probably won't be

28

too bad, Shep. You never know. Maybe this . . . What's her name . . . McDonald?"

"Montgomery."

"Maybe this Montgomery woman feels weird about it, too."

Tess had a way of preaching sometimes. Sheppy knew she was only trying to help, but it bothered her anyway.

"So how's camp?" Sheppy asked.

"The same, so far. Same cabins. Same counselors. Same food."

The same. How could it be the same? If Sheppy had been the one to go and Tess had stayed home, it wouldn't be the same. Sheppy would be miserable. She was miserable now.

"I guess you're having a good time then."

Silence.

"Well, yeah, so far," Tess said. "But it would be more fun if you were here, of course."

Of course.

Sheppy could hear a girl in the background calling Tess's name.

"Who's that?"

"Roberta. She's one of my roommates. I guess I have to go now. We're getting ready to go hiking, and Mom said I could only talk for a few minutes, especially if it was a weekday."

"Okay," Sheppy said.

"Good luck today," Tess said. "I'll write."

"Me, too."

"Bye."

"Bye." Sheppy felt a tightness in her chest. Why? Her best friend had called all the way from camp to wish her well, so why did she feel so crummy? So mad?

"Wasn't it nice of Tessa to call?" Mama said from the pantry. "Is everything all right with her? She must miss you."

"Yes" was all Sheppy could say.

She wanted to be asked if everything was all right with *her* and if *she* missed anybody.

Sheppy went into the kitchen and poured corn flakes and milk into a bowl. Papa had loved corn flakes. Kellogg's corn flakes. She wanted to say, "Mama, remember how Papa would only eat Kellogg's corn flakes, and how we put another brand in a Kellogg's box to test him and he knew right away that they weren't Kellogg's?" Instead she crunched and studied the list of chores attached to the refrigerator door.

- Run sweeper
- Dust
- Sort laundry
- Scrub bathroom tub and sink
- Clean toilet bowl (good for one breakfast in bed)
- Sweep kitchen floor
- Scrub kitchen floor

She was tempted to add to the list: Don't talk about Papa.

"When are you doing the laundry, Mama?"

"Sheppy, if you have something that you want washed, you're going to have to do it by hand. I'm not the family maid, you know."

"That's not what I meant, Mama," Sheppy said. She tried to hide her frustration. "I just wanted to know if I should sort laundry now or after I get back."

"Oh." It was quiet for a moment.

Then Mama came into the kitchen and said, "Why don't you just go on upstairs, straighten your room a bit, and get ready for Miss Montgomery." She touched Sheppy's arm. "I could do your hair. Would you like that?"

"Sure, Mama," Sheppy said. "Where's Ranger? Isn't he supposed to be taking me over there?"

"He'll be here. He left early to cut grass. Said it wasn't too big a job, so he'll be back in time."

Maybe he wouldn't get back, she thought, hoped. Maybe she wouldn't have to start today. *This is dumb.* Miss Montgomery was just a lady. And it was only three hours. So what was she so nervous about? And who was she kidding? Always reliable Ranger would be perfectly on time.

He was.

"Made it," he said as he came in the door. He was wet with sweat, but still looked clean. Ranger always looked clean.

Sheppy had just finished tying on her Keds.

"Let me take a look," Mama said, signaling her to turn around. She winked at Ranger. "Looks like a working girl to me."

He nodded his agreement.

Sheppy didn't know what they meant. Mr. Montgomery had told her she didn't have to dress up. So she was only wearing jeans, though her nicest ones, and her red button-down shirt. And Mama had fixed her thick hair into a French braid. It was nice and tight. Neat looking. Clean. Like Ranger.

Sheppy wondered what Papa would've said. He'd probably have found a poem about a working girl. She almost said so, but stopped herself.

"Ready, Miss Lee?" her brother said in a singsong voice.

"Ready!" Sheppy sang back, trying to piggyback on his enthusiasm. Then she added, a little less music in her voice, "I guess."

Chapter 7

"I know you'd rather be at camp than doing this," Ranger said as he started the car.

"Yeah, well, that's the way it goes," Sheppy said. She rolled down her window and looked out. The sun was bright and hot, but there was a coolness in the air.

"You know if I had the money I'd . . ."

"Forget it, Range. Anyway, it's not your fault." *Whose fault was it?*

"It's nobody's fault, Shep," he said, as if he'd heard her thoughts.

Then silence. More silence these days than she had ever known. Not just with Ranger, but everybody.

Ranger pulled into the Montgomerys' driveway and stopped the car. He turned to Sheppy and smiled. His smile had changed. It had always seemed easy, comfortable. Now his eyes showed the effort. *Smile for her,* they said.

"Break a leg."

"Very funny." She got out of the car.

"See you at three," he called after her.

Sheppy checked her watch. 11:50. Was it okay to be early? The door opened before she could ring the bell. Sheppy stood eye to eye with a tanned woman in a crisp, yellow dress. The woman took Sheppy's arm and pulled her inside.

"You must be Mary. Come right in. I'm Mrs. Fletcher. I'm so glad you're on time."

Sheppy smiled, nodded, and was led through the house and into the kitchen before the woman ran out of breath.

"I'll always leave instructions regarding Constance's lunch." Mrs. Fletcher pointed to a note on the counter, then picked up her purse and opened the back door leading out of the kitchen. "If anything needs to be heated, don't use the microwave. She won't eat it." She stood holding the door open for a second, thinking, as if she might be forgetting something. Then she said, "I'll be back by three," and left.

Sheppy watched out the window as the woman walked across the yard. Part of Sheppy felt relieved Mrs. Fletcher was gone. Part of her wished she had stayed to explain things more.

The instructions were only about lunch.

- Heat vegetable soup (in pan in fridge)
- Serve with wheat toast or saltines (in cupboard above toaster)

34

- Fruit cocktail (in bowl in fridge)
- Cottage cheese (in fridge)
- Iced tea (already prepared in pitcher in fridge) or hot tea (tea canister on counter) or milk
- (Dishes in cupboard above sink. Silverware in drawer to left of sink)

Pretty dull eating. The kitchen was spotless, just like everything else. Mrs. Fletcher hadn't even taken the time to show her around, to introduce her to Miss Montgomery. Maybe she thought they had already met. Suddenly Sheppy had to go to the bathroom. But where *was* the bathroom? She would have to do some exploring.

Her instincts led her to a powder room off the kitchen. Everything was so sparkling clean, Sheppy couldn't bring herself to wash her hands in the marble sink. She used the sink in the kitchen instead, drying her hands on a paper towel.

Then she remembered something. She had to see that laundry chute. She opened the door and found it wasn't a laundry chute at all, but a small elevator for sending things to and from the second floor. She couldn't remember what they were called, but she'd seen them in old movies. She smiled at the discovery. Tess would love this.

As she stood with the elevator door open, Sheppy heard voices from upstairs. She listened. A television was on. She closed the door and took a deep breath. There was no way to avoid it. She was here to do a job. She had to go upstairs and meet Miss Montgomery. Then she needed to find out when to fix lunch.

The stairs angled at a landing halfway up and at the top there was an expanded hallway with books and a desk, like a small library. Though there were a number of doorways, the sounds from the TV were coming from a room across from the bathroom. Sheppy knocked lightly on the half-closed door and said, "Miss Montgomery?"

Silence.

"Miss Montgomery?"

"Come in," the woman said. Then she muttered, "I can't stop you," in the sharp voice Sheppy'd heard through the elevator door a week before. Sheppy froze for an instant, then entered the room.

"Sit," Miss Montgomery said and pointed to a chair next to the bed. Sheppy immediately thought of Tess and their dog game. For a second, she felt like barking and had to concentrate on keeping a straight face.

The woman didn't say anything else for a few minutes. A long few minutes. She seemed interested in something on the TV news. Constance Montgomery was thin as a ballet dancer, her dark brown hair woven into one long braid and twisted into a bun at the back of her neck. Her voice had made her sound older, but she was young. Except for her eyes. They were gray, surrounded by dark circles. Gray, like a fossil stone when it's wet. Ancient gray.

A cast covered her right leg and was resting on some pillows. She sat propped up with more pillows behind her back, and looked uncomfortable, like she needed one of those bendable electric beds they had in hospitals.

Finally Miss Montgomery cleared her throat and said, "What's your name again?"

"Sheppy, ma'am. Sheppy Lee."

"A nickname, I suppose."

"Yes, ma'am."

"What's your given name?"

"Mary Sheppard, ma'am."

"Mary Sheppard," the woman repeated to herself like she was deciding whether or not she liked it.

"When would you like your lunch, ma'am?"

"Must you say that?" Miss Montgomery continued to look at the television screen. She seemed annoyed.

"Excuse me, ma'am, but I don't know what you mean?"

"There. You did it again," she said with a huff. "All that ma'aming."

Sheppy wasn't sure how to reply. Finally she said, "Mama and Papa always said it's a way to show respect."

"Well, I'm nobody's ma'am," Miss Montgomery said, sitting up and punching the pillows a few times. Was she fluffing them up or pretending to hit somebody? "I suppose you've been calling my uncle *sir?*" she whispered, as if it were a bad word.

"Yes, ma'am. I mean, I'm sorry. I don't know what to call you now."

Silence.

Finally Sheppy asked, "Should I call you 'Miss Montgomery'?"

"Not unless you expect me to call you 'Miss Lee.' The way I see it, if I have to call you a ridiculous name like 'Sheppy,' then you'll just have to call me 'Connie.' "

It would be strange. Sheppy wasn't used to calling adults by their first names. But she smiled.

"Except of course when my uncle or that neighbor woman is present. Then you must use my surname as you have been." She picked up the TV remote and flicked the channel. "Now, I'm hungry. And *All Our Lives* is on."

Sheppy laughed. "Mama calls it 'All Our Problems.' "

The woman stared at her, unblinking. Then shifted her eyes to the television screen.

"I'll get lunch," Sheppy said, uneasy again.

Back in the kitchen, she realized she'd forgotten to ask Miss Montgomery whether she wanted toast or crackers, milk or tea. And did she want fruit and cottage cheese or just soup? There was no way Sheppy was going back up to ask, so she decided to serve some of everything. That way Miss Montgomery could eat what she wanted. To keep from spilling the drinks, Sheppy carried the meal up to the library in two trips. Then she put everything on a wicker tray with legs.

"What in the world?" Miss Montgomery said when Sheppy placed the tray over her lap. "Are you planning to share my lunch? I can't think of any other reason for all this food."

"No, ma'am. I mean, Connie. I wasn't sure what you'd want and . . ."

"Ever heard of asking?"

"I'm sorry I . . ."

"Shhh!" Miss Montgomery waved the back of her hand as if dismissing Sheppy and focused again on the soap opera.

Sheppy went downstairs. Her eyes stung, and it was hard to keep from stomping. She sat at the kitchen table, wishing she had her library book. Wishing she could be reading it . . . at home or at camp with Tess.

After a while a bell rang from upstairs and she went up. Miss Montgomery motioned her to take the tray away, and Sheppy returned to the kitchen and cleaned up. Then, so she'd be nearby if needed, she sat upstairs in the library hallway, afraid to touch any of the books without permission. Afraid to ask.

For the rest of the afternoon the woman watched soap operas. Didn't say another word to Sheppy, except when she needed to use the bathroom.

"Please come here, Sheppy," she called.

Sheppy went in and stood next to the bed, while Miss Montgomery used her hands to swing her broken leg over the side.

"Take me across the hall," she said, using a cane to support her good side and leaning the weight of her cast side on Sheppy's shoulder.

Sheppy had watched Ranger helping Papa to the bathroom those last weeks, so she knew what to do. Give as much support as possible and don't move too fast. The cast seemed heavier than the body attached, as if everything Constance Montgomery was had been drawn into it. Eerie. Like it was some creature in a science fiction movie. Sheppy slid her arm around the tiny waist and Miss Montgomery leaned heavily against her, using the cane for balance. With Miss Montgomery hopping on her good leg and Sheppy walking beside her, they slowly made their way across the room.

Moving around in the bathroom was awkward, but finally Miss Montgomery was seated on the toilet. Then Sheppy realized that she might need to help more. She remembered that Mr. Montgomery had said she shouldn't be squeamish.

"Will you need help with anything else?" Sheppy asked.

Miss Montgomery looked puzzled a second, then Sheppy added, more quietly, "Your underpants maybe?"

A hint of a smile appeared on Miss Montgomery's face. "I'm not wearing any. Thought it would make things easier."

"Oh," Sheppy said.

"I'll call you when I need to go back."

Sheppy nodded and shut the door. Closed her eyes and took a deep breath. Then she smiled. Miss Montgomery had come up with a sure-fire way to avoid panty raids. Don't wear any.

Chapter

8

"Any problems?" Mrs. Fletcher asked when she returned a few minutes after three. "That's good," she said before Sheppy could open her mouth.

"Miss Montgomery didn't eat much," Sheppy said.

"She never does. Don't worry about it. Personally, I think she does it just to worry Charles. Uh, Mr. Montgomery. Getting back at him for . . . Well, that's none of your business, now is it?"

Where was Ranger? Sheppy wanted to leave.

"You just do your job here and don't ask questions. We . . . Mr. Montgomery knows best."

Sheppy heard Miss Montgomery's bell ring again.

Mrs. Fletcher sighed. "I'll get that." She started up the stairs. Then stopped and smiled. "Tomorrow at noon. You were punctual today. That's good. Keep it up."

Something inside Sheppy wanted to see to Miss Montgomery herself. Mrs. Fletcher didn't seem to really want to take care of her. But had Sheppy?

Honk!

Ranger. Thank goodness.

"You're late," Sheppy said when she got in the car.

"Ten minutes, Shep. So, sue me." He pulled away from the house fast.

There was that silence again.

"Hey, I didn't mean anything," she said, touching his arm. "It's just not like you, that's all. You're usually early." She leaned over and kissed his cheek.

"Yeah, well, I . . ."

"You don't have to explain."

He glanced at her and smiled. "Thanks. So how was your first day?"

"Okay. But a little weird."

"What's your patient like? Old and crabby?"

"No, she's young. She wants me to call her Connie, but only when we're alone. And she hardly talked to me. Just watched soap operas all day."

Ranger laughed. " 'This could be the beginning of a beautiful friendship.' Movie line."

"*Casablanca*. Humphrey Bogart. I wonder if I could get her to start watching old movies."

"Or maybe she'll get you hooked on the soaps."

"Ha!" Sheppy settled back in her seat. Ranger was Ranger again.

• • •

"Sounds like you did just fine," Mama said when she'd heard about Sheppy's first day.

"Sure, Mama. I guess so," Sheppy said. It was what her mother wanted to hear. But what Sheppy hadn't said was how uncomfortable Miss Montgomery had made her feel, that it seemed like she didn't want her there. Something wasn't right with her. Mrs. Fletcher, too. It must have shown on Sheppy's face because Mama said, "I know what you need." Her face looked full of mischief when she pulled an envelope from the back pocket of her pants.

"A letter from Tess? She didn't mention a letter this morning."

Sheppy started to take it, but Mama pulled it out of reach and said, "Guess again."

Sheppy was disappointed. She thought a minute.

"I don't know. Who?"

Mama handed her the envelope. Sheppy read the return address. *Parker Ford, Box 501, R.D. #2, Leslie, West Virginia.*

"Parker," she said quietly, looking at the envelope. He had never written to her before. Except teasing notes in class.

"Maybe he's feeling homesick," Mama said. "It's amazing what a little distance can do."

Sheppy was dying to read the letter, but not with Mama there. She shrugged and said, "I'm hungry."

Mama frowned. "Didn't you eat at the Montgomerys'?"

No, Sheppy hadn't eaten. In her first-day nervousness,

eating had been the last thing on her mind. She didn't want to worry Mama, so she said, "I'm just hungry again. Maybe I'll take a peanut butter sandwich tomorrow."

"Well, there's tuna salad," Mama said. "I'll fix you a sandwich."

The phone rang, and she picked it up. Sheppy looked again at the envelope in her hand.

"I'll be right there," Mama said into the receiver.

Someone from the Laundromat. For once Sheppy was glad that Mama was leaving. She put the letter in her pocket.

"You'll have to make your own sandwich, honey. Sorry." Mama kissed her on the cheek and headed for the door. "I won't be long."

"Bye."

Sheppy made a sandwich, poured a glass of iced tea, and went to her room. She tore open the envelope. Ranger always cut his open with scissors or a knife so the opening was straight and neat. Sheppy didn't get many letters, but the ones she had looked like they could have been opened by a gorilla. She didn't care. Just like with a book or a person, it wasn't the condition of the envelope that mattered, but what was inside. Papa had taught her that.

Dear Germ,

I guess you never expected to hear from me again. Well, this may turn out to be the first and last time you or anybody else hears from me. If you read in the paper about a kid who disappeared into the nothingness of Leslie, you'll be able to say you knew me. Leslie is a town (Can I call it a town?) that exists only for the people who are unlucky enough to live here.

The day after we got down here, the miners went out on strike. Dad could work, but he'd have to cross the picket line and probably get beat up, and there's no other work here. There's nothing here but nothing, and nobody here but nobodies.

My dad always plays old records by the Beatles. They're old now and one of them's dead and they're not together anymore, but they were a pretty good band, and some of their lyrics are cool. Anyway, in this one song called "Nowhere Man" they talk about a guy who sits around planning stuff for nobody. That's us. We're nobodies going nowhere, me and my dad.

I couldn't tell you or anybody this before, but my mother (can I still call her my mother?) left. She said she needed to find out some things about herself and she had to be on her own to do it. She told me I'd be better off staying with Dad. I heard him crying tonight, and I guess it's what made me write this letter. I think maybe she wants a divorce. I hate her. I'm not sure why I picked you to lay this on, but I figured you might understand with your dad gone and all. In a way, you're lucky. Your father didn't leave on purpose.

Lucky? She didn't feel lucky. And what Papa had gone through. That wasn't lucky. How could Parker say that?

Anyway, I got your address from the graduation directory. I didn't know who else to talk to about it. Aunt Ella, Dad's sister, and Uncle Hank seem okay, but things are crowded here, and I can tell it's making everybody crazy. They all go around joking and acting like everything is just as wonderful as a day at Kennywood Park. Do grown-ups think we're stupid or what?

I can't stand to hear Dad crying. Sheppy, remember I said there's nothing to be scared of? I take it back.

Parker

P. S. It's okay if you don't write back.
P. P. S. What kind of music do you like?

Poor Parker. That was why Mrs. Ford wasn't at graduation, why Parker seemed so sad. Sheppy had never heard Papa cry, but sometimes she could tell he was hurting inside. From his eyes. And the way he held his mouth. How could Mrs. Ford just leave like that? Mama never would. Never.

And why couldn't Parker have written his best friend?

46

That's what Sheppy'd have done. He had always hung around with the same two kids at school. Why hadn't he told one of them?

Sheppy knew she had to write him back. But what could she say?

Chapter 9

Sheppy took a deep breath and walked into Miss Montgomery's bedroom. "I brought our Scrabble game from home. I thought maybe you'd like to play. Mama says when your body isn't cooperating, at least you can exercise your mind."

"I don't play games," Miss Montgomery said, keeping her eyes on the television screen.

"Oh," Sheppy said quietly. She had finished cleaning up after lunch and now it looked like another afternoon of soap operas. Just like the past three days. *Yuck!*

She sat down and put the game on the floor beside her. On the TV a woman and a man were stranded in a log cabin. The woman was getting ready to have a baby, and the man was nervous because he was a magazine editor, not a doctor.

Sheppy wondered if there was something good on the

classic movie station. She loved the old black-and-white movies. Like *Roman Holiday* with Audrey Hepburn and Gregory Peck. She thought of her book, too. She had started bringing one with her the past few days, but never got much time to read. Miss Montgomery always wanted Sheppy to watch TV with her.

A commercial came on and Miss Montgomery sighed the way Mama did sometimes after Sheppy'd been nagging her about something. A giving-in sigh. "Can you show me how to play your game while we watch my programs?"

"Yes, ma'am! I mean, Connie," Sheppy said. "We can play during commercials. It's not hard." She picked up the game, happy that two Christmases before Mama had bought them the deluxe version with the little plastic slots for each letter. Sheppy set the board on the tray Miss Montgomery used for lunch.

"Do you ever do crossword puzzles?" Sheppy asked.

"Yes."

"Well, in Scrabble you're kind of making a crossword puzzle without the clues." Papa had explained it to Sheppy like that.

A small line formed between Miss Montgomery's eyebrows as though she was thinking. Then the story came back on and she turned back to the TV.

Sheppy placed all the wooden letters facedown in the box lid while she waited.

Friday night had always been game time at home. Monopoly, 500 rummy, Password, jacks, Scrabble. It was as regular as Papa's bowling night, Mama's card club, and choir rehearsal. Even after Ranger had started dating Hayley, they would often go out for a while, but end up back at the house. At first Sheppy wondered if it bothered Hayley. But she fit right in and became like one of the family, arguing about the rules and laughing, adding to that noisy, wonderful time.

They took turns choosing the game for the evening. Mama was the best at Scrabble. She knew all kinds of strange words, like YURT, because she did crossword puzzles all the time. She read a lot, too. Papa liked 500. When they played, they never stopped at 500 points. They just kept on playing until they didn't feel like playing anymore, sometimes until after midnight. But Friday nights had been empty of games since . . .

"Go on. I'm listening." Miss Montgomery turned toward Sheppy again. A commercial had come on.

"We each pick seven letters to start and we put them on these racks so the other players can't see them," Sheppy said. "The rules say you're to draw letters to decide who's first, but you can go first."

"No," Miss Montgomery said. "If I'm going to play this game at all, I want to play by the rules."

"Okay, we each draw a letter and whoever picks the one closest to A goes first."

Sheppy drew D. Miss Montgomery picked L.

"I go first."

"I know. I'm not an idiot."

"I didn't mean . . ." Sheppy started to say, but Miss

Montgomery waved her hand and said, "Let's just get on with it."

Sheppy couldn't help smiling to herself. It served Miss Montgomery right. She couldn't just let Sheppy be nice. *She* wanted to play by the rules.

"Now we put these letters back in the box and draw our seven letters," Sheppy explained.

By the time they'd gotten their letters, the soap opera was back on.

Sheppy didn't really mind. She used the time to study her letters. I O T E A I K. She could make TEA or TOE or TAKE or KATE. No, KATE was a proper name. She would make KITE instead. She waited until the commercial. At this speed they could be playing the same game of Scrabble all summer. But she didn't care. As long as they were doing *something* fun.

When the commercial came on, Sheppy said, "Okay, now we take turns using the letters we have, but all the words have to connect like they do in a crossword puzzle." She put her word on the board. "Except the first one, since there aren't any words to connect to.

"The first word on the board has to cross the pink star square in the middle." Sheppy pointed to the number on the T in KITE. "Each letter is worth points. You just add them up and keep track of your score. After each turn, you pick enough new letters so you'll have seven again. Whoever has the most points when all the letters are gone is the winner."

She counted her points. "Oh yeah, something else. It looks like my word is worth eight points, but it's really worth sixteen because it crosses a pink square. Pink means you can double your points for the whole word. And see, some let you double or triple points for one letter." She pointed to a red square. "This is the best. A *triple* word score!" She made her voice sound enthusiastic to help get Miss Montgomery into the game.

"Why are some letters worth more points than others?" Miss Montgomery asked. Sheppy was glad for the question. It showed she was interested.

"Things like vowels and Ts are only worth one because they're in lots of words. But an X or a Q is harder to use and there's only one of each, so they're worth more."

"Interesting," Miss Montgomery said, looking at the box lid with all the letters turned facedown. "Like people. We're faceless, valueless, equal in a way, until somebody sees what's underneath. The sad thing is that even after the unveiling, some remain valueless."

The commercial was over, but she looked back at the board and said, "You could see it the other way around, you know. Those that are needed more often are in higher demand and, therefore, more valuable."

Sheppy didn't quite understand what Miss Montgomery was getting at, but what she said reminded her of something.

"You should know that there *are* two letters that are blank," she said. "They're not worth any points, but you can make them any letter you want. Like a wild card."

"Ha!" Miss Montgomery startled Sheppy for a second. "So the blank ones might have more value than any of the others. I like that!" She laughed, but she didn't sound happy.

It was quiet for a while. Miss Montgomery just sat there looking toward the window.

Finally Sheppy said, "It's your turn," hoping to get things going.

It worked.

Miss Montgomery made TUNE using the T in Kite. She only got four points.

Sheppy made FADE from the E in TUNE and got another double word score. Sixteen points again.

The soap opera came back on. Sheppy sat back. Miss Montgomery wouldn't be taking her turn for a while.

If Tess was playing she would be going crazy. She couldn't stand it when Sheppy took a long time to place a word. But Sheppy usually won, because she knew how to make good use of the bonus squares. That was why she sometimes took a little longer.

Tess. Sheppy wondered what her friend was doing at that very moment. Hiking? Horseback riding? Swimming? Being friends with someone else? Sheppy had gotten a postcard from her the day before. It was short, but you couldn't fit much on a postcard.

The picture on the card was the main lodge and the big bear statue that stood outside. The same postcard Camp Walking Bear sold for the past kazillion years. On the back, Tess had written:

Dear Sheppy,

The lake is freezing cold as usual, but the weather has been great. No rain. Yet. I went riding today. Bullet's still here, so I rode him, of course. Roberta, one of my bunkmates, went with me. She rode Sugarfoot. Guess what she calls him? "Shug." Hope your job is okay. Write me.

Love, Tess

Shug. It was what Sheppy had called her favorite horse. Who was this Roberta anyway?

Commercial.

Miss Montgomery had a blank square. She put it at the end of TUNE to make TUNES, then added AME to make SAME. She got nine points, but Sheppy saw right away that Miss Montgomery could have done the same thing at the end of KITE and gotten a lot more points. When she was first learning to play, Papa used to show her stuff like that. It helped her learn to look for the best move.

"If you move here to make KITES, you'll get more points," Sheppy said, "because . . ."

"I see," Miss Montgomery said. "But are other players supposed to tell each other that sort of thing?"

"Oh, well, no," Sheppy said. "I just thought that since you were just learning the game, and I don't mind."

"Well, *I* do," she said firmly. "If I make mistakes, then that's my problem. I lose. Isn't that the way things work?"

Sheppy didn't say anything. Decided it was best just to take her turn.

She added an S to KITES and made SAW for twenty-three points.

The story came back on, but Miss Montgomery took her turn anyway. She used the M in SAME to make MAY, for sixteen points. She looked pleased. Sheppy was glad.

Sheppy put an H over the E in SAME and got ten points because it fell on a double word box.

Miss Montgomery made APRIL using the A in FADE. *Uh, oh.*

"I wouldn't say anything," Sheppy said carefully, "but you said you wanted to know the rules."

"Yes, what now?"

"Well, you can't use APRIL because it's a word that's capitalized. I forgot to tell you that you can't make words that are proper names, abbreviations, or words from other languages."

"Then why didn't you say anything about MAY?"

"Oh," Sheppy said, "I guess I thought you meant the other may. You know, like *may* I have a cookie or something?"

"I see. I guess you could think that," Miss Montgomery said frowning.

Silence.

"I'm getting tired," she said flatly. "I think I'd just like to watch television now."

"Okay," Sheppy said. She put the game away.

They didn't talk much the rest of the time, and when she helped Miss Montgomery to the bathroom, Sheppy's heart wasn't in it. She lost her balance and almost made them both fall.

Later Sheppy went downstairs to make sure she'd remembered to put everything away in the kitchen. Then she sat in the living room and closed her eyes.

She shouldn't have brought the game. It hadn't made their afternoon better as she had hoped. It had made things worse. Maybe the people who made Scrabble should be required to put a warning on the box: Not Recommended When Trying to Make Friends.

Chapter 10

Sheppy watched from the window as Mrs. Fletcher rushed off with hardly a word, her backside moving from side to side. Why wouldn't someone who always seemed to be in a hurry wear looser clothes?

The note about lunch was the same as it had been every day for the past week except that canned pineapple chunks were substituted for fruit cocktail. No wonder Miss Montgomery didn't eat much.

Sheppy opened the door to the little elevator and listened. The news was on. Except for that awful Scrabble day the week before, she felt like she was in the *Twilight Zone,* stuck in a time warp where she kept reliving the same day. Same menu. Same TV programs. Same Miss Montgomery. She closed the door and went upstairs.

The bedroom door was open. Sheppy stopped at the entrance and tapped lightly on the wood of the door frame.

Miss Montgomery looked over at her for a second, nodded, then fixed her eyes back on the television screen.

"Hello . . . Connie." Sheppy sat in the chair next to the bed. "What would you like for your lunch today? There's soup and . . ."

"I know what there is and . . . just a minute," she said. The anchorman was saying something about a ninth grader who had killed his parents.

"That Tom Regent," Miss Montgomery said. "He can say a thing like that and not even blink an eye. Doesn't he wonder what would make a child do such a thing?"

"Stay tuned for *All Our Lives*," Tom Regent said.

"Just give me some of the fruit, whatever it is, and some cottage cheese and crackers. I suppose they're those awful saltines again?"

Sheppy nodded.

"Well, bring them along."

"What would you like to drink?"

"Iced tea with one sugar and two lemon wedges."

Sheppy smiled to herself. It should be the other way around. Constance Montgomery could do with a little extra sweet and a little less sour.

In the kitchen Sheppy thought about the newscast. Parker had said he hated his mother. Could he ever hate her enough to . . . She didn't even want to think about it. She needed to write him soon. Didn't know how, but maybe she could help.

She took the iced tea up first, then the tray with food as

she had been doing all week. Today she'd almost tripped while carrying the food up the stairs.

"You can use the dumbwaiter, you know," Miss Montgomery said during a commercial.

That's what the little elevator was called, a dumbwaiter. Sheppy remembered now. "Oh, can I?" She'd been wanting to since her first day.

"No, you can't. I just thought I'd say that." Miss Montgomery shook her head. "What is wrong with you? I just said you could, didn't I?"

"Yes, ma'am. Connie, I mean. Thank you."

She'd known what Sheppy meant. Why did she have to act so mean?

The story came back on. The man and woman were still stuck in the cabin and the woman was still waiting to have a baby. Sheppy was glad when Miss Montgomery finished her lunch, so she could go down to the kitchen and clean up.

"How does the dumbwaiter work?" Sheppy asked.

"Blue button, up. Red button, down."

Sheppy went out into the hall and opened the little door. The shaft was empty. She pushed the blue button and heard a motor start. Soon a platform boxed on three sides appeared. She put the tray on the platform, closed the door, and pushed the red button. When she got downstairs, she opened the door. There was the tray. Pretty cool. She allowed herself a few minutes to enjoy this new experience. It might be the only bit of fun her summer job would offer.

She removed the tray and pushed the blue button. The platform went up. Then she pushed the red button to bring it back down again.

Sheppy washed the dishes, then sat at the kitchen table and ate the sandwich and apple she had brought from home with some milk from the Montgomerys' refrigerator. She had started bringing her lunch after the second day when she'd told Mama about the boring food at the Montgomerys'.

After lunch, she took her book, *Words by Heart,* from her purse and went up to the library. Miss Constance Montgomery would just have to watch TV by herself. Sheppy sat in a chair and flipped the pages to her place. The book was the last one that Papa had added to their Everlasting Reading List. Hers and Papa's. They were always adding new books to it and crossing off ones they'd read, so it went on forever. When she heard about a good book, she'd tell Papa and they'd add it to the list, and he'd do the same. They read them together, taking turns reading out loud. Papa had books that he read by himself and so did Sheppy, but this was a list they shared.

Words by Heart by Ouida Sebestyen was one that Papa heard about from a librarian. He'd said it was about an African-American girl who was very close to her father and that it took place in the past. Sheppy liked stories from the past. And Papa always said it was important that she learn about black people. But she'd chosen it mostly because it was a book about a girl and her father.

One night, during his last weeks, Sheppy was reading to

Papa from Lloyd Alexander's *The Book of Three* and he'd said, "While I'm sick, it's going to be up to you to keep the Everlasting List from ending." *While I'm sick*. Papa knew he would never get well. But he wanted Sheppy to keep believing.

She had kept reading books from the list, but she hadn't added any. Not since Papa'd added *Words by Heart*.

Sheppy found her place in the book. Little Roy had just spilled milk all over Mrs. Chism's book. The one Lena had borrowed without asking. Sheppy still couldn't believe Lena had taken the book. It was 1910. Didn't she know that she might be lynched for even a little thing like that? Then Lena lied about it to her father. Well, she didn't lie outright. She just didn't tell the truth, which is the same thing. Had Sheppy lied to Papa those last weeks? Lied to herself? She'd kept believing in the possibles. That stupid poem *Anything can happen, Papa. Anything can be*. It wasn't true.

Were all lies the same, or were some kinds of lies okay? The kind that maybe made somebody else feel better. Or maybe gave somebody hope, even if there was none.

"Sheppy!"

Her body jerked in reaction to the voice. "Yes." She went into the bedroom. Sheppy felt tears on her cheeks. She hadn't realized.

"What are you doing out there?" Miss Montgomery asked. She didn't sound hard, just curious.

"Reading," Sheppy said, quickly wiping her face with her hand.

61

"There was a time in the South when it was illegal for black people to read. Did you know that?"

"Yes. My fa . . . yes." She was going to say her father had told her about it but was afraid if she tried to say all that she'd start crying again.

"Are you unhappy about being here?"

"No, ma'am." A lie. But she couldn't chance losing her job. Mama would be upset. This kind of lie had to be okay.

"What are you reading?"

"*Words by Heart.*"

The woman reached over and Sheppy handed her the book.

"What words? What does it mean?"

"Bible verses," Sheppy said. "Lena, the main character, knows hundreds of Bible verses by heart. She wins a contest. She beats a white boy, and it makes some people mad."

"Is that what you were crying about? This book?"

"No. Well, yes, I guess in a way."

"Well . . . make up your mind."

Sheppy could feel her eyes start to fill again. "Excuse me, ma'am, but . . ." *Ma'am.* She'd said it again. Before Miss Montgomery could react, Sheppy turned and left the room.

Downstairs she threw herself into a chair in the living room. Why did Miss Montgomery have to talk to her that way? What was she so mad about? Sheppy got a Kleenex from the powder room and blew her nose. She looked at the clock. 2:46. Fourteen minutes. She gathered her purse and quickly looked around the kitchen to make sure everything was clean and in place. She looked at the clock again. Thirteen minutes.

A bell rang upstairs. No! Sheppy didn't want to go back up there. Not today. The bell again. Louder. Miss Montgomery might really need something.

Sheppy took a deep breath and set her purse on the table. As she started up the stairs, she heard the kitchen door open and stopped. Mrs. Fletcher was back. Sheppy could let *her* deal with Miss Montgomery. The bell rang again and Sheppy heard Mrs. Fletcher saying, "What does she want now?" as she clicked over the hardwood floor through the living room toward the stairs.

"I'll see," Sheppy heard herself say. Suddenly, she felt a need to protect Miss Montgomery from this woman in the too-tight dress.

"Yes, you're still on duty, I suppose."

Sheppy hurried up the stairs, two at a time. When she reached the bedroom door, she realized she didn't want to go in after all. Didn't want to deal with either of the two women.

She straightened her back, walked stiffly into the room, and stood next to the bed like she'd seen servants do in movies. "Is there something you need?" She'd almost said, "ma'am" again but caught herself.

"You forgot your book," Miss Montgomery said, handing it to her. "I thought you might read at night . . . in bed. And you'd be without it."

"Oh," Sheppy said. The stiffness left her. "Thanks." She

started to leave but felt uncomfortable. She wanted to do something for Miss Montgomery. "Umm. Do you have to go to the bathroom or anything before I leave?" She couldn't think of anything else to offer.

"That would be a help," Miss Montgomery said.

Sheppy put the book on the night stand and took her around the waist. The bathroom routine seemed to get easier each time, like they were learning to dance.

As Sheppy was returning her to bed, Miss Montgomery asked, "You don't like soap operas, do you?"

Should she lie?

A car horn sounded. Ranger.

"I have to go now," she said. "My brother is here. I'll see you tomorrow." She turned to leave but stopped at the door with her back to Miss Montgomery. "No, I guess I don't like soap operas. I'm sorry," she said and walked out.

There. She'd told the truth. Would it set her free like people always said?

Chapter 11

"What happened to the car?" Sheppy asked, getting in. A headlight was broken. Silence. Ranger drove away from the house and out onto the street.

"What happened?" Sheppy said again.

"Nothing," he said flatly, his eyes never leaving the road ahead.

He was soaking wet with sweat, his face streaked with dirt. Always clean Ranger. Suddenly Sheppy was scared. She spoke carefully, almost in a whisper.

"Range, it's not that bad. Mama won't be too mad."

Still, he didn't look at her. Just kept driving, like she wasn't even there.

Sheppy sat back in her seat and turned her head toward the window. The passing world blurred. Where were the tears coming from? Didn't a person ever run dry?

Mama wasn't home when they got there.

Sheppy watched her brother, his feet dragging heavily on each step as he went upstairs and into the bathroom.

She quietly followed him up and stood by the bathroom door. The sound of water running in the sink. And something else. Crying. Not just crying. Sobbing.

What was the matter? She wanted to be with him. To hug him. Help him somehow. But something told her to leave Ranger alone.

Sheppy went into her bedroom and lay on the bed. She thought of Parker, listening to his father cry. Her body felt heavy, ached. She pulled her knees up to her chest and wrapped her arms around them. Closed her eyes and forced herself to think of nothing. Blank white paper. White paper. White paper.

• • •

"Sheppy."

She opened her eyes and rolled over. She'd been sleeping.

"Hi, Mama."

"Are you feeling all right?" She held her hand to Sheppy's forehead. "It's not like you to sleep in the middle of the day."

"I feel fine," Sheppy said getting up. She tucked in her shirt.

Mama looked at Sheppy's face. "Sure you're okay?"

"Yes, Mama." Another lie. "Where's Ranger?"

"He called me at the Laundromat and said one of the car

headlights wasn't working. Wanted to have it looked at before the mechanic closed. Harvey brought me home," Mama said as they went downstairs to the kitchen.

Typical Ranger. He couldn't completely lie to Mama. But Sheppy was sure he'd left out that the headlight was broken.

"Would you peel some potatoes for dinner?" Mama asked, gesturing toward the sink.

Sheppy nodded and washed her hands.

"How was work today?"

"Okay. You know that little door we saw at the Montgomerys' house? It's not a laundry chute, it's a dumbwaiter."

Mama smiled. "Well, there aren't many of those around anymore."

"I used it today for Miss Montgomery's lunch," Sheppy said cutting a potato in half. "Pretty neat."

"Not quite as much fun as horseback riding at camp, though," Mama said, a sadness in her voice.

"It's okay, Mama," Sheppy said. "There's always next year . . . maybe."

The door opened. Ranger. Sheppy forced her eyes to stay focused on the potato she was peeling.

"Hi!" She heard him say. He sounded okay. But how did he look?

She turned to see him hug Mama and kiss her cheek. He was his old clean self again, and smiling, but his eyes still weren't right.

"Hey, sis, your fan club is growing," he said, waving two envelopes in the air.

"Two?" Sheppy dried her hands on a dish towel and reached for the letters. Ranger held them above his head and read, "Tessa Clark and this one's from . . . Parker Ford?"

He looked at Sheppy and raised an eyebrow. "Didn't you get a letter from him last week? Sounds like this could be getting serious." He turned to Mama. "Mother, we may have to have this guy checked out. Make sure his intentions are honorable."

Sheppy jumped up trying to snatch the letters from his hand, but he was too tall.

"Ranger! Come on."

He laughed and lowered his arm so she could reach. Sheppy wanted to go to her room and read the letters right away, but she slipped them into her pocket and went back to peeling potatoes.

"I'll finish there, honey. You go on and enjoy your mail."

"Thanks, Mama," she said, "but there's just a couple more."

Ranger walked out of the kitchen and upstairs, whistling the theme from the movie *Romeo and Juliet*. Sheppy's face flushed. It wasn't like that with Parker. People always thought that just because a boy and girl were friends there was some kind of romance going on. But that wasn't what bothered her. Ranger was only kidding and she wanted to be glad that he was his old self again. But she knew it wasn't real. Ranger was acting. They all were.

Sheppy cut the potatoes in chunks and put them on the stove to boil, then set the table.

"Go on now," Mama said, turning the chicken she was frying. "I'll call you for dinner."

The sound the bedroom door made when Sheppy closed herself in was a relief. She tore open Tess's letter first.

Dear Sheppy,

It's supposed to be RT, but RT isn't rest time anymore at Walking Bare. At least not in our cabin. RT has become riot time. You wouldn't believe the people I'm bunking with. They aren't the types to read or write letters.

Rhonda talks really loud and swears. She's always talking about how much she hates school and how dumb camp is.

Sue is on another planet. Even though it's against the rules, she brought her Walkman and plays it anytime the counselors aren't around. She keeps it hidden in her backpack. When she's not spaced out listening to music, she's singing . . . well rapping. That's the kind of music she likes.

Roberta likes to read, like us. (Thank goodness.) And she also likes movies. She talks about them a lot and always knows what stars played what characters. Kind of like you. She loves the Safety Pack. She wears a *real* bra. Not like the stupid training kind we have. I let Roberta put the two she brought in my Pack. Maybe your mom could go into business selling UP Safety Packs to campers all over the world!

The ink changed from blue to black.

It's almost lights out time. I had to stop writing before because RT was over and Roberta was bugging me to go riding.
Write me. Have to go.

Love, Tess

Sheppy could hardly believe Tess had let a total stranger use her Safety Pack. And Tess had been as excited as Sheppy about getting their bras this year. Now suddenly she was calling them "stupid." So what if this Roberta wore a *real* bra? So what.

Chapter 12

The first thing Sheppy noticed when she opened Parker's letter was that it was short. The second was that he didn't call her Germ.

Dear Sheppy,
   I was thinking about what I wrote in my first letter, and I wanted to say I'm sorry for saying you're lucky. I know you don't feel very lucky. I didn't mean to hurt your feelings. I was just thinking about my own problems. I don't blame you if you're mad, but please don't be. I'm sorry.
                                                    Parker

It was okay. She wasn't mad. It was nice of Parker to think of her feelings. Maybe she'd get another letter from

Tess, too, apologizing for never even once saying she missed Sheppy.

In the meantime, she had to write Parker. Sheppy looked in her desk. She was out of paper. She went downstairs.

"Mama," she said peeking her head into the kitchen. "Do you have some paper I could use to write a letter?"

"I think there's some kind of writing paper down in your father's office. Look in one of the left-hand drawers of the desk." Mama was taking chicken pieces from the skillet. It smelled so good, Sheppy wanted some right then.

"When do we eat?"

"In a bit," Mama said. "Here's a sample." She pulled apart a wing and handed Sheppy the largest section.

"Thanks!"

Mama made the best fried chicken. Sheppy ate the chicken and dropped the bone into an empty milk carton on the sink. "Hey, maybe we could sell your chicken, Mama. Go into business. Then you wouldn't need to work for somebody else."

Mama laughed. "I think the Colonel has that market covered."

"That's just because nobody but us knows about yours."

"Thank you, baby," Mama said. "Now go on down and get your paper. Sounds like you have at least two important letters to write."

Sheppy nodded, wiping her hands on a tea towel.

In the basement, she wondered how long it had been since anyone had been in Papa's office. Maybe he was the last person to have been there.

The office was small and narrow. It used to be the fruit cellar before Papa remodeled the basement into a game room.

The wall above the desk was covered with photographs, all of which she had seen many times before. Papa and Mama sitting on the rocks at the beach. Ranger at five dressed as a cowboy for Halloween. Ranger with Sheppy on the porch steps. Mama with Sheppy on the porch steps. Mama sitting on Papa's shoulders. Papa with some Navy buddies. Papa in a nightclub with the great blues musician B. B. King. He was so proud of that picture. Grandmother and Grandfather Lee at the beach, Grandma and Grandpa Berry by the tulips in their yard. Sheppy sitting on Papa's knee. Already she'd forgotten what it felt like, sitting on his knee.

And, there was the family picture that Papa had taken with the self-timer last Christmas. Mama and Papa sitting on the piano bench with Ranger and Sheppy standing behind. They were all smiling. Who would have known that it would be their last Christmas together? Who would have known that there was something horrible there with them? The cancer. It wasn't right—to sneak up on people like that.

She turned away from the pictures. Didn't want to look anymore. What had she come here for? Paper.

Sheppy reached down and opened the bottom drawer. There were some tablets and folders stacked inside. She pulled out the tablet on top. The pages were yellow with age and there was writing inside. Papa's writing. Then Sheppy realized that she'd opened the right-hand drawer instead of the left. She put the tablet back and started to close the drawer but couldn't. Couldn't close it on Papa. Seeing his handwriting had made her feel odd. Like he was there. She took out the tablet again and opened it.

First Love

She was barely six,
and I was only seven.
She was my sweetheart,
and boy was I in heaven.
I was kinda bashful,
and she a little shy.
But we caught love's golden arrow,
when we caught each other's eye.

Nice. Sheppy smiled and turned the page.

Sunday Dinner

Chicken on the stove,
Greens in the pot,
Biscuits in the oven
Pipin' hot.
Wild buttered rice,
Gold-yellow yams,

Sweet corn on the cob,
There's honey and jam.

It's Sunday
and Daddy's home.

Sheppy had heard this one before. Papa used to recite it sometimes. He had liked the poem so much he'd copied it down, but like "First Love" the author wasn't named. Papa must have had trouble remembering all the words because some had been crossed out and replaced with the right ones.

Sheppy looked at the poem again. There was another part to it. She remembered now. Maybe . . . she turned the page. Yes, there it was.

After Sunday Dinner

Playin' poker,
Drinkin' mountain dew,
Talkin' and laughin'
and swearin' too.
Just a bunch of friends
with nothin' to do,
on a hot Sunday afternoon
after dinner is through.

Mama!
Preacher's comin'!

Papa hadn't shared this one with Sheppy until about a year ago. He'd probably thought that, before then, she'd been too young to hear about drinking and swearing and gambling.

"What's wrong with drinking Mountain Dew?" Sheppy had wanted to know.

He'd laughed, hugged her and said, "Nothing, baby. Nothing."

Sheppy could tell there was something he wasn't saying. Later Ranger explained that mountain dew used to mean moonshine. "You know, homemade liquor that people cook up in a still?" he'd said.

At dinner she'd said, "I know what mountain dew is, Papa."

"That's fine," Papa'd said. "Just as long as you don't know what it tastes like." Sheppy could hear him saying it in her mind, but it wasn't clear. As if the memory of his voice was fading. Would she someday forget the sound completely? She closed her eyes and listened for Papa's voice again. It was still there. No, she could never forget.

Sheppy turned the page. Another poem. "The Shut-In." This one was initialed "N.E.L." N. E. L. Norris Edward Lee. Papa.

Her mind flashed back to the first time he'd recited "Sunday Dinner." She flipped back to it.

"Who wrote that one?" she recalled asking.

"Can't seem to remember," he'd said. It wasn't like Papa to forget a thing like that. Now, seeing it written by his own hand, Sheppy knew he hadn't forgotten. Papa was the poet. Papa. It made sense now. He hadn't forgotten words in the poems. He had changed his mind about them. Had liked the sound of "Pipin' hot" better than "Steamin' hot," "Playin' poker," better than "Playin' cards."

Papa had read many poems to her and knew some by heart. But always other people's poems. At least, that's what Sheppy had thought. But why hadn't he told her? Why hadn't Mama?

She went back to "The Shut-In."

The Shut-In

I wanna go places.
I wanna see
the people . . . their faces.
I wanna be
there,
to share
the fun and joy
of all the things I've read about
since I was a boy.

I would have loved
to've caught the fish
that's on my dish,
to explore
the ocean floor
and what's more,
to encounter some old sea monster,

amongst other things,
would have been my dream.

To cross the open desert
on a camel's back
with just a little sack
of . . . whatever they eat.
And perhaps to meet
or get to know
the kinds of folks
you go there to see
who are people . . . like me.

Had Papa felt shut in? Was he unhappy?

"Everybody needs to have dreams. Like the trees need sunshine," Papa'd said. "We need something to reach for. Direction. And just like the trees we have to be patient. To give ourselves time to grow."

At the time, Sheppy couldn't think of a dream to reach for. She remembered feeling uncomfortable about it. Like she was the only person in the class who didn't know the multiplication tables. When Papa had said it, all Sheppy had wanted was for him and Mama to take her and Ranger to get ice cream. But that wasn't what Papa meant. That wasn't a dream. Ranger's music. That was a dream. Sheppy wanted something important like that to reach for. But somehow she couldn't think that far ahead.

She read the poem again. How many of *Papa's* dreams had come true? Had any? God hadn't given him much time. It wasn't fair.

"Sheppy! Dinner!"

She wiped her face with the bottom of her tee shirt. She didn't want dinner.

Papa. She wanted Papa.

Chapter

13

"Mama, I found something down here. Can you come down?" "Hey, Range, come and see what Papa wrote!" Sheppy thought of calling them, but stopped herself.

"Sheppy!"

If Mama knew about the poems, maybe there was a reason she hadn't told Sheppy. If she didn't know about them, did Sheppy want to show her? What if they made her cry? And Ranger. He used to be the first person she shared things with. But she didn't know what was going on with him. Maybe it was better to keep the poems to herself for now.

"I'm coming!" she called.

Sheppy returned the tablet to the drawer and closed it. She opened a drawer on the other side. Paper. She grabbed some.

On her way to the stairs, she stopped to look in the mirror in the game room. Awful. Anybody could tell she'd been crying.

"I'll be there in a minute, Mama. I have to go to the bathroom," Sheppy said when she got upstairs. She washed her face and forced a smile at herself in the mirror. *I was only seven . . . boy, was I in heaven,* ran through her head. She smiled a real smile. Maybe she *should* tell them.

• • •

At dinner Mama asked, "You were downstairs a long time. Did you find the paper?"

"Yes, ma'am. I, I was just looking at stuff."

"Hmm. I thought something wasn't right with you. Those pictures."

Sheppy bit her lip and looked at her plate.

"I know, honey. Something of you wants to look at them, and something of you doesn't."

Sheppy looked up and nodded. Mama's eyes glistened.

"Excuse me," Ranger said. He dropped his napkin beside his plate and left the table.

Mama's gaze followed him out of the kitchen. A familiar vertical crease formed between her eyebrows. Her worry line.

She reached over and squeezed Sheppy's hand. Mama took a bite of chicken leg and ate in silence. After a moment she asked, "Do you really think we could beat the Colonel?"

Sheppy wanted to scream. She played along, saying,

81

"Sure, Mama," but hated the game. Mama's change of subject was Ranger's fault. She might have talked, really talked, about Papa. It felt like she was going to. Sheppy might have even told about the poems. But Ranger had to go and spoil it by walking out. As if to say, "I can't handle talking about Papa, so nobody can talk about Papa." *Well, maybe some of us can't handle* not *talking about him.*

Mama and Sheppy finished their dinner in silence, and Mama started clearing the table. She covered Ranger's plate with aluminum foil and put it in the refrigerator.

It was Ranger's turn, but Sheppy said, "I'll do the dishes, Mama. You rest."

Mama touched Sheppy's cheek, smiled slightly, and went upstairs.

Sheppy felt good to be helping Mama, but it was hard to keep from slamming a few pots around. She resented doing Ranger's dishes. How did Papa's poem go? *I wanna go places . . .* She took a deep breath and counted to ten.

• • •

Dear Parker,

I'm not ready to write this letter, but I didn't want you to think I was mad. I'm not.

I'm sorry about your dad's job and about your mother.

Don't be scared. The Beatles weren't talking about you in that song. You and your dad aren't nobodies going nowhere. You're somebodies. Things will work out. I can't say how, but they will.

I guess I'm not helping much, but I'll think of something, I promise. I'll write again soon.

Your friend, Sheppy

She read the letter over, just before turning off her light. Sheppy knew she shouldn't promise, but she had to give Parker something. He needed *something*. A promise was the best she could do for now, even if it turned out to be a broken one.

She lay in bed and looked out her window. Sheppy had come to see the moon as a wonderful thing. Its soft light made her feel safe from the dark.

But tonight, there was no moon.

Chapter 14

It was as if the tablet were a huge magnet. The poems. They were down there pulling at her. Sheppy hadn't gone back to the basement after dinner because she didn't want a lot of questions. But she couldn't fight it anymore. She needed to go back. Back to Papa.

The house was quiet and dark except for the night light Mama always left on in the hall so they could find their way to the bathroom. Sheppy didn't turn on her flashlight until she reached the stairs. She moved as if in slow motion, shushing herself softly as she made her way down to the living room. She followed the beam of the flashlight to the basement door. The door squeaked slightly when she opened it. She stopped for a moment and listened. Had anyone heard? She looked down the stairs. Pitch black. Then she heard something. Something throbbing in her ears. *Ba-Boom. Ba-Boom. Ba-Boom.* Her heart-beat. And Sheppy knew she couldn't do it. Couldn't face this darkness by herself.

Tomorrow. She'd get the tablet tomorrow.

Chapter 15

"Sorry about yesterday," Ranger said while driving to the Montgomerys'.

What did he mean? Was he sorry about leaving the table at dinner? About not talking to her in the car? About crying?

"So what was going on? What *is* going on?" Sheppy asked.

His face said, *please don't ask me.*

"You used to tell me things. I'm worried about you, Range. And I miss you."

He looked straight ahead at the road and said, "I just need some space right now. Can you give me that, Shep?"

She leaned her head against the seat back. It was hard knowing he was keeping something from her. But she had secrets of her own. Sheppy had hoped to get to the basement before she went to the Montgomerys', but things hadn't gone as planned. She'd thought that maybe while Mama was opening the Laundromat and Ranger was still sleeping or in the shower, she could slip downstairs. But Sheppy had forgotten to set her alarm, and Mama was home by the time she got up.

"Shep?"

"Okay, Ranger. I'll try."

. . .

Mrs. Fletcher opened the door before Sheppy had a chance to ring the bell.

"You're late," she said angrily. "You people are going to have to learn that you won't keep a job if you can't be on time."

Sheppy felt her face get hot. *You people*. As she followed the woman into the kitchen she looked at her watch. 12:04. It was because she'd gone back to the house to get some leftover fried chicken for her lunch.

"We won't tolerate tardiness. Is that clear?" Mrs. Fletcher said, balancing on red, sandal-like high heels, her chubby feet oozing out the sides. "I don't want to have to tell Charl . . . , uh, Mr. Montgomery about this."

"Yes, ma'am. I mean, no, ma'am."

The woman stared at Sheppy for a moment, grabbed her purse, and left. There had been something hanging from one of Mrs. Fletcher's nostrils. If it had been Mama or even Miss Montgomery, Sheppy would have offered a Kleenex or found some other nice way to tell her. Mama always said it was best to let a person know that his fly was open or there was food stuck in his teeth. She said it would save more embarrassment later. But Sheppy didn't do a thing to warn Mrs. Fletcher. Not one thing.

• • •

There was chicken noodle soup for lunch and canned peaches. Poor Miss M. *Miss M.* Sheppy liked that. Maybe Miss Montgomery would like it, too.

She opened the dumbwaiter door and listened. Strange. No television today. She went upstairs and stood in Miss Montgomery's doorway.

The woman looked up from the book she was reading.

"Come in, please," she said.

It wasn't until Sheppy sat down that she realized. *Words by Heart.* Miss Montgomery was reading *Words by Heart.* Sheppy remembered putting it down to help her to the bathroom the day before.

"It's all right, isn't it?" Miss Montgomery said, holding the book up. "I haven't read a book in ages and, well, I found it here after you left."

Sheppy didn't know what to say. It felt like Miss Montgomery was asking her permission.

"Sure," Sheppy said. "How far did you get?"

"Mrs. Chism wants to send Lena's father to Hawk Hill to repair fences, but Papa doesn't want to go. He's told Lena it's because he doesn't want to be away from the family, but Lena knows that Papa doesn't feel comfortable taking work from Mrs. Chism's other hired man, Mr. Haney. Haney deserves it, since he hasn't been doing the work. But he's white and that makes him think he's better than Lena and her father."

"Did you get to the part where little Roy spills milk all over . . . ?"

Miss Montgomery waved her hand in the air. "Don't tell me."

Sheppy almost laughed out loud. It was something she'd often said herself. To Tess.

"Maybe I should get lunch while you read."

"I'm not very hungry today."

Sheppy felt it was her job to make sure Miss Montgomery ate something. She was so skinny.

"You should have *something*. How about some soup today with wheat toast?" She tried to make it sound yummy, but who was she trying to kid?

Miss Montgomery's face showed her lack of interest.

Then Sheppy got an idea. "If I bring you something different, something you might like, will you be hungry then?"

"And just what do you have in mind?" asked Miss Montgomery, raising an eyebrow.

"Just wait and see. It's a surprise. I'll be back."

Downstairs Sheppy took the fried chicken breast from her lunch bag. She pulled the meat from the bone and put it on a plate. She opened the refrigerator and looked in the vegetable drawer. Good. Lettuce. There was a jar of mayonnaise on a shelf above. As she closed the refrigerator, her eye caught two tomatoes on the windowsill. Should she use one? She ran upstairs.

"Do you like tomatoes?"

"Why yes."

"Would it be all right if I used one?"

"Of course. I do live here, you know."

"Yes, ma'am. Miss M, I mean. It's just that it's not on Mrs. Fletcher's list and . . ."

Miss Montgomery's eyes went cold. Sheppy tensed. She shouldn't have called her Miss M. It just slipped out.

"That woman does *not* run this house," Miss Montgomery said. She took a deep breath as if to rid herself of the anger that had overcome her. Maybe she was counting to ten.

"I would love tomatoes with whatever you're preparing, Sheppy. Thank you," she said.

Downstairs Sheppy hummed to herself as she toasted two slices of wheat bread and spread one with mayonnaise. She carefully put pieces of chicken on the mayonnaise side, then two slices of tomato, some lettuce, and the top piece of toast. She put the sandwich on a plate and cut it in half, point to point like Mama always did. It looked a little lonely all by itself. Needed something on the side. Some chips maybe. Sheppy felt uneasy snooping into cupboards, but figured it was okay since she was looking for something for Miss Montgomery. Canned food, cereal, crackers, rice, spaghetti, pretzels. Pretzels!

She moved the sandwich to the center of the plate and surrounded it with pretzels. She stepped back and looked at it. Too many. She took one off. Perfect. She ate the pretzel.

She placed the plate on the tray with a glass of iced tea

and a napkin and set it in the dumbwaiter. Blue button, up.

"It's a chicken sandwich," she said, setting the tray over Miss Montgomery's legs. She felt the familiar dampness under her arms. A combination of excitement and worry.

"Well," Miss Montgomery said, "look at this." She was smiling. A big smile. "Where did you get the chicken?"

"My mother fried it yesterday for dinner. I brought a piece for my lunch."

Miss Montgomery looked concerned. "Your lunch. I can't eat your lunch."

"It's okay. I want you to have it. Really."

"It looks very good."

"Taste it," Sheppy said.

Miss Montgomery took a bite and closed her eyes. She chewed slowly and began nodding her head.

"Delicious! Delicious! Are the pretzels yours, too?"

"No, I found them in a cupboard downstairs."

"Hmmm," she said biting a pretzel. "I wonder what else Uncle Charles has down there that he's not sharing with me?" She crunched a moment, then asked, "So what are you having?"

Sheppy hadn't thought about it. "Well, there's a little chicken left and the rest of the tomato. I'll have something later."

"No, get it now and bring it up."

• • •

After lunch, Sheppy cleaned up, putting everything back where she had found it and then went back upstairs. As she helped Miss Montgomery to the bathroom, Sheppy asked, "Miss M?" Sheppy studied her carefully to catch a reaction to the name. She saw the corner of Miss Montgomery's mouth turn up slightly. It was all right. She finished her question. "I was just wondering. How did you break your leg?"

Miss Montgomery didn't answer until Sheppy had returned her to bed. "If you must know, I fell down the stairs. But it isn't something I care to discuss."

"Oh, okay," Sheppy said nervously. "Hey, it's almost one o'clock, past time for *All Our Lives*. Should I turn it on?"

"No, just come and sit down." Miss Montgomery patted the arm of the chair beside her. "I've read *Words by Heart* up to your bookmark, and I do want to know what happens."

There was a long pause. What did she want Sheppy to say? That she could keep the book until she finished? That she would tell her how it came out? Then Sheppy guessed.

"Maybe we could read it out loud?"

"What a good idea," Miss Montgomery said. It seemed it was exactly what she wanted. But why hadn't she just said so? Was she being shy? Constance Montgomery shy?

"Would you like to read or should I?" Sheppy asked.

"What if we take turns? That way nobody's voice gets too tired."

"Okay, but I'll go first, since I'm supposed to be taking care of you," Sheppy said.

"Very well."

They picked up at the part where Lena's Papa said she had led him to think a lie.

"I want so many things, Papa. So much."

"I know you do, baby girl. But you have to get them the right way. I want things for you, too. For all of us. And sometimes I'm tempted. Lord knows I am. But we'll help each other hold out. All right?"

She moved toward him hesitantly along the fence. "All right."

The sun rose out of a cloud bank, as lifegiving as his smile.

. . .

Just a few minutes later, or so it seemed, Sheppy heard the door open downstairs. Mrs. Fletcher. Could it be three o'clock already?

Darn. Sheppy stopped reading.

Miss Montgomery put a finger to her lips. "Shhhh, maybe she'll go away."

Sheppy put the bookmark in.

"Should I tell her about lunch? About the tomato?"

"No," Miss Montgomery said, "I'll tell her. Please, keep reading until your brother arrives."

Sheppy looked at the clock. 2:58. The day before she'd counted the minutes because she'd wanted to leave. Now she counted the minutes because she wanted to stay. She wanted to stay. And Miss Montgomery wanted her to. But Mrs. Fletcher had broken the spell, and now she heard the car horn.

She looked at Miss Montgomery.

"I know," she said. "Go on now. I'll see you tomorrow."

"I'll leave the book here if you promise not to read ahead."

"Cross my heart," she said, smiling.

And *"The sun rose out of a cloud bank, . . . lifegiving . . ."*

Chapter 16

Sheppy watched Ranger drive away from their house after dropping her off. He'd said he had something to do before he picked up Mama from work. What was going on in his head? In his heart? She wanted to pound it out of him. But she'd promised to give him space.

She turned away from the kitchen window wishing for their old closeness, yet glad finally to be alone. She could get the tablet now.

First she read Mama's note on the refrigerator. It was about dinner.

- Meat loaf in at 3:30.
- Macaroni and cheese at 4 o'clock.

She turned the oven on to preheat and ran to the basement.

At the door to Papa's office she paused. As though she

were about to enter some holy place. The feeling hadn't been there the day before. Had she been disrespectful then?

She sat carefully in Papa's chair, opened the drawer, and pulled out the tablet. There were others underneath. Should she take those, too? No. One at a time. Should she take *any*? Suddenly she was being watched. She felt it. All the eyes in the pictures. Holding the tablet tight against her, Sheppy ran upstairs to her room. Papa always said things happened for a reason. If she wasn't meant to read the poems, she wouldn't have found them. She lay across her bed and opened the tablet.

> *Everyday I seem to find . . .*
> *Some of you . . . you left behind . . .*
> *Something little . . . not very much . . .*
> *Just a bit of your personal touch . . .*

When did Papa write this? And who was the "you" in the poem? An old friend, someone he knew a long time ago? Someone who had died?

The next page in the tablet was blank. There were some hand-drawn musical notes, and Papa had written *Ranger* at the top of the page and then a list of song titles. But Papa and Ranger wouldn't call them *songs*. They usually said *compositions* or *pieces*. Sheppy recognized some of them, like "When Sunny Gets Blue" and Beethoven's Moonlight Sonata. And there was Rachmaninoff's Prelude in C Sharp, the one Ranger had been practicing so hard for his auditions. Ranger had told her how to pronounce it many times—*Rock* something. But Sheppy could never remember, so she just called it *Rocky's C Sharp*.

Mama said once that Papa had dreamed of becoming a musician, too, but his parents never encouraged him. They thought he should do something practical, so he became an auto body repairman. His customers said he was an artist when it came to rebuilding cars. His doctors said years of dust and paint and chemical fumes had probably given Papa lung cancer.

If only you could see a person on the inside, see how certain things affected his lungs, his liver, his heart, maybe you could do something to protect him. Like with hands. People wear gloves when they're working in the garden, cleaning the oven. Ranger wore them every day when he did yard work. Sometimes Papa wore gloves when he worked, too. Still, his hands were hard and rough with callouses. His fingers had been short, thick, but they didn't stop him from beating everyone at jacks. Or from playing the piano.

Sheppy closed her eyes and remembered. "Rhapsody in Blue." Some nights, Papa played it as she lay in bed. The music worked its way up the stairs and rocked her to sleep. Sometimes the music would end and Sheppy'd think hard, *Once more, Papa. Please.* And soon it would start again. Somehow he'd gotten her message. "Rhapsody in Blue." She missed that. Would never hear him play it again. Why hadn't she ever thought to turn on their little cassette recorder while he was playing? But why should she when she believed she would have the real thing every day of her life? And even if she had thought to tape him, could she stand to listen to it now?

How empty of music the house had become. Papa used to play every day. Ranger, too. Sometimes Ranger played a song over so many times, Sheppy carried it around in her head all day and almost felt as if she knew every note herself. But that hadn't happened in a long time. Ranger wasn't playing. Sheppy'd heard him start to play a couple of times, but after a little while, he'd bang the piano keys like he was mad at somebody. He was supposed to practice every day. Papa'd said so. Why wasn't Mama saying so now?

Sheppy looked back at the tablet and turned the page.

> *Will you love me in the springtime?*
> *Will you love me in the fall?*
> *Will you love me when the moon's a-shining,*
> *Or when there ain't no moon at-tall?*
> *Will you love me when I'm down and out,*
> *And when I'm old and gray?*
> *Will you love me, love me, madly?*
> *Every day in every way?*

Sheppy remembered this one. Why hadn't she guessed then that it was his? Papa had recited it in the hospital, after she had shared the Shel Silverstein poem. When Papa'd said, "Will you love me, love me, madly?" Sheppy'd said, "Gladly." And Papa'd hugged her and said she was a poet. She'd wondered for a moment if poetry could be for her what music was for Ranger. Something to reach for. But just then, her only dream had been for Papa to get well.

She read Papa's poem again. Ranger would like the part about the moon. Sometimes when the moon was full, he would play the Moonlight Sonata on the piano. Then he and Sheppy would sit on the porch swing and sing every song about the moon that they could think of. "Blue Moon," "By the Light of the Silvery Moon," "Mr. Moonlight," "Harvest Moon." After they ran out of ideas, they'd start singing the same ones over again.

Mama'd call out the kitchen window, "Can't you kids sing something else? The neighbors must be getting tired of those."

Then Papa would look out through the screen door and say, "I know one," or "How about 'Moon River'?" Then he'd start singing. And Mama would join in, too. Sometimes even the neighbors would come out. Because the moon was magical. It brought people together. She and Ranger needed that now.

More blank pages followed, then another poem.

Are you ready to die?
Are you ready to go?
If you had no choice,
and you couldn't say no?
Could you give it all up
with a wink of the eye,
and say, "Lord, take me
I'm ready to die"?

Can you go right away
and leave all behind?
Can you meet your Maker
with peace of mind?
Can you go as you are
and not ask why?
And mean it when you say
that you're ready to die?

Was Papa ready? How could he have been? Why would God take him when she needed him here? God had His choice of millions of people. She only had one Papa. Sheppy laid her head facedown into her pillow to muffle a sob. She turned over and closed her eyes. She tried to think of blank paper, but words kept appearing on the whiteness: "Are you ready to die?"

"Are you ready to die?" A big hand came down out of the sky, through the clouds, and Papa walked toward it. Sheppy grabbed his hand and tried to pull him back. "No, Papa! No! You're not ready! You're not!" Then there was thunder and lightning and . . .

Sheppy jerked awake. She felt shaky, scared. Usually when she had bad dreams, she'd go to Mama. They'd talk about it, then Mama would stay in Sheppy's room until she went back to sleep. But Mama wasn't there, and it was the middle of the day. And . . .

The meat loaf! Sheppy checked her watch. Almost four

thirty. She closed the tablet, slipped it under her pillow, and ran downstairs.

She put the meat loaf in. The macaroni and cheese would be done before the meat loaf if she put it in now, too. She'd have to wait until five o'clock. Shoot! Dinner would be late. The timer had been right there on the counter by the stove. She should have set it when she'd turned the oven on.

Papa had bought that old timer after they'd first made cookies together. They kept forgetting the time, letting the cookies burn. They'd eaten them anyway, but the next day, Papa came home with the timer.

He set it on the counter and said, "Timing is important. In cooking. In speaking. In athletics. In music. In love. In life."

And what about death? How many years of fumes had Papa inhaled before it was too late? Did God know? Had He been counting? Keeping time? When does the timer go off? At the point of no return or at the end?

If only you could see a person on the inside. Papa had kept his writing private. And those last weeks, he hadn't shared his pain. Like Ranger now.

If only you could see a person on the inside. Before his time was up.

Chapter
17

"Pass the pepper please," Ranger said.

Sheppy handed it across the table, holding on for a second, trying to make him look at her. He glanced up, but didn't meet her eyes. He had probably focused on her forehead. In school when they did plays or had to recite, the teachers always said if you looked at the heads of the people in the audience you'd be less nervous and it would appear that you were looking right in their eyes.

Sheppy studied her brother closely. He was thinner. He was moving food around his plate but not really eating, even though meat loaf was his favorite. He wasn't the same. Anybody who knew Ranger before would know. Mama should know. Maybe she, too, had promised to give him space. Or maybe she just hadn't noticed. Mama looked tired. Today she had opened the Laundromat, gone to clean someone's house, then gone back to the Laundromat to check on things before coming home. Home to a late dinner.

"Sorry about dinner, Mama," Sheppy said for the fourth time.

Mama gave her a stern look, but her eyes seemed playful. "If you tell me you're sorry one more time, you're going to be." Then she looked at Ranger, but spoke as though to Sheppy. "I know what can happen when you get your mind on something else."

"Thanks, Mama. May I have some bread, please?"

She passed Sheppy the basket. "The woman I worked for today told me there was a burglary at one of the Beacon Heights homes last night," Mama said. "Did either of you hear anything about it while you were up there today?"

"No," Ranger answered, keeping his eyes focused on his plate.

"Miss M didn't say anything," Sheppy said.

"I thought it might be one of your lawn customers," Mama said to Ranger.

"I don't know. I didn't hear," he said.

But he *did* know. Something. Sheppy could tell. She looked at him, puzzled. Her eyes must have asked *What's going on?* because Ranger's eyes shot back at her. *Back off.*

Her stomach turned over. No. Not Ranger. He was the one who'd never pick apples from Cook's trees even though they just went to waste. Mr. Cook didn't want kids on his property, so it was trespassing to be there, and

Ranger always said it would be stealing to pick the apples. He was so good. Sometimes it made Sheppy proud to be his sister. Sometimes it made her mad.

He cleared his throat. "So did you get another letter from that Ford guy? Isn't he that white kid who bugged you in class all the time?"

Sheppy swallowed her food too fast and said, "So what if he's white?"

"So nothing," Ranger said. "Just be careful, that's all. Sometimes those guys are just looking to brag to their friends. Like it's some kind of status symbol to have a black girl. Like it shows they're cool or something."

Who *was* this? Not Ranger. "First of all," she said, pressing her index fingers together for effect, "Parker is *not* my boyfriend. Second, even if he *was,* so what? And, third . . . third . . ." her voice got loud. "You don't know anything about him."

He looked at Mama and said, "Tell her that I'm right."

"Ranger, you know we don't talk like that in this house," Mama said firmly. Then she closed her eyes and sighed. She put her elbow on the table and held her forehead in her hand. "I wish you two wouldn't argue."

Sheppy kicked Ranger under the table and glared at him. *Look what you've done to Mama.*

His face softened. Suddenly he looked uncomfortable, sorry. He reached out and gently touched them both. "Forget it," he said softly. "I'm just blowing off steam. Don't pay any attention to me."

Sheppy shuddered. A minute ago he was being a jerk, now he wanted to make up. Jekyll and Hyde. She had to get away from him.

"Excuse me," she said and marched upstairs to her room. He could do the dishes tonight. But slowly Sheppy felt her anger turn to a cold chill. Ranger had brought up Parker to get away from Mama's questions about the burglary.

·   ·   ·

Dear Tess,

My papa always said that family stuff should stay in the family. I don't feel right breaking that rule, but there isn't anybody else to talk to. I don't want to upset Mama. She's working real hard and is tired a lot. I know she misses Papa. And I can't talk to Ranger. I can't believe I'm saying that, but it's true. I'm scared for him. I'm not sure what's going on, but something is. I can't explain it. But I think he's doing something wrong.

His buddies William and Roland are away for the summer working for Roland's uncle at his lumberyard somewhere in Vermont. And remember Ranger and Hayley broke up? I don't think he's seeing anyone new yet. He seems so alone right now. He's not even practicing his music. I want to help, but I don't know what to do.

I wish you were here.

Love, Sheppy

Why tell Tess? Because she always kept Sheppy's secrets. Because it somehow helped to know that Tess knew. But that was before. Tessa was probably too busy at camp with her new friends to care much now.

Sheppy read the letter over. Funny how putting a thing in writing changes it. Makes it be. But it couldn't be true. What was she thinking? Doing? She felt like she was walking on the ceiling, trying to grab onto something below and pull herself back to normal. Would anything ever be normal again? . . . *doing something wrong.* No matter how things seemed, Sheppy knew her brother. There had to be an explanation. She had promised Ranger space. To trust him.

She tore up the letter and threw it in her trash can.

"Shep?" It was Ranger, knocking on her door.

"C'mon in."

"Look, I'm sorry for what I said about your friend. I don't know what's wrong with me." He sat on her windowsill.

"It's okay," Sheppy said. "Are you in any trouble, Range?"

He didn't answer.

"I know I promised not to ask any more questions, but I can't help it."

He hesitated, then said, "I'm doing something for Mama. For us."

"But . . ."

Ranger put his finger to his lips. "Don't worry. I can handle it. So, what about you? Is everything okay? With your friend Parker? And how's Tess?" He turned her desk chair around and straddled it.

He was changing the subject again. But she let it go. At least they were talking. Sheppy sat on the bed.

"Tess is fine, I guess. She seems to be having fun without me."

"Impossible," Ranger said in his old, wonderful, familiar way.

Sheppy laughed. It felt good.

"And Parker?"

"Well," she said, "he's having some problems at home. He needs a friend and, for some reason, he picked me."

"Smart guy," Ranger said.

"I don't know. I want to help, but I don't know what I can do." She had said the same thing to Tess about Ranger.

"Just be you, baby sister," he said walking out the door. "Just be you."

Sheppy fell back on her bed and hugged herself, full of love for her brother, but uneasy about what he was hiding.

Chapter 18

Sheppy stood in Miss Montgomery's bedroom doorway. "Do you like meat loaf, Miss M?"

Miss Montgomery looked up and frowned. "People do whatever they wish. It doesn't seem to matter what I want," she said sharply.

Sheppy felt a tightness in her stomach. Amazing how a few words could change a person's mood in an instant. Alakazam! And not just words, but how a person said them.

"Did I do something wrong?"

"I told you to call me Connie, didn't I?"

"Yes, ma'am. I mean, Connie. I'm sorry," Sheppy said quietly, but she didn't understand. The day before, she had called her *Miss M* twice and Miss Montgomery didn't seem to mind. Or had Sheppy dreamed the day before? She looked at the hardwood floor and focused on a circular design in one of the boards. It was beautiful. Simple.

"Sheppy?"

"Yes?" she said, keeping her eyes locked on the center of the circle.

"Why *Miss M?*" The woman's voice was less harsh.

Still Sheppy stayed with the comfort of the wood. "Well," she said, "Connie's a nice name, but it seems strange for me to call you that. You're a grown-up. I mean, my parents, my mom wouldn't approve. But Miss Montgomery doesn't feel right either. It's a lot to say and not as friendly. Miss M is somewhere in the middle."

Miss Montgomery didn't say anything for a while. Finally she said, "All right, Miss M it is."

Sheppy looked up, still uncertain. "Are you sure? I could try harder to call you Connie."

"It's growing on me. Besides, there are already too many things to be stumbling over. A name shouldn't be an obstacle."

Miss Montgomery seemed okay again. But Sheppy would have to be careful. The woman could turn from light to dark in an instant. Like Ranger. Was it some kind of epidemic?

"I *do* like meat loaf," Miss Montgomery said. "Is that what we're having for lunch?"

"If you want."

"Your mother's?"

Sheppy smiled and nodded. "Would you like it in a sandwich or just on a plate with something on the side?"

"In a sandwich with tomato. Any fruit today?"

"Cantaloupe."

"Sounds good."

On the way down the stairs, Sheppy thought of something and called back, "Would you like the meat loaf cold or heated?"

"Heated, please. Just use the microwave."

"But Mrs. Fletcher said . . . never mind."

"Sheppy?"

Uh, oh. "Yes?"

"Please, come back here."

Sheppy went back up the stairs and stood in the doorway.

"What did Mrs. Fletcher say?" The tightness was back in her voice.

Sheppy didn't want to say. Didn't want to chance making her angry again. But she didn't have a choice.

"Only that you somehow could tell when something was cooked in the microwave and that you wouldn't eat it."

Miss Montgomery smiled. "Oh, I see." Then she started chuckling and waved Sheppy off. "I will eat it if *you* use the microwave. Go on now and fix us lunch."

Sheppy didn't get the joke, but didn't really care. The main thing was that Miss Montgomery wasn't mad.

• • •

"Look at that," Miss Montgomery said, pointing at the TV. "Tom Regent just said that a house on this street was burglarized two days ago."

"Mama mentioned it yesterday," Sheppy said, hoping her discomfort didn't show. *Change the subject.* "Would you like anything else?"

"No, thank you. It was delicious," she said, wiping her lips with her napkin. No. Not wiping them. Dabbing her lips. Gently.

"We'll read when you come back," Miss Montgomery said as Sheppy carried the tray to the dumbwaiter.

. . .

She loved listening to Miss Montgomery read. Sheppy could close her eyes and see everything that was happening. Like when Papa read.

Miss Montgomery read about the white boy, Winslow, who had been in the contest with Lena at the beginning. Lena had remembered more Bible verses than Winslow. Now he wanted to be her friend, but his father said he couldn't because Lena was black. *Negro* was the word they used then. He wouldn't even look at her now. Lena felt bad, but you could tell he did, too. It wasn't right for the grown-ups to keep them apart.

She wondered if Parker's father knew that he and Sheppy were friends. If he knew, was it okay with him? *Words by Heart* happened a long time ago, but Sheppy knew that some people were still like Winslow's father.

Mrs. Fletcher's remark about being late still stung. *You people,* she'd said. People were people, Mama and Papa always said. Sheppy's race was part of what made her Sheppy, but only part. She didn't carry it around in her conscious mind on a regular basis. Not the way she carried her awareness of being a girl or being a kid. So Mrs. Fletcher had taken her by surprise, caught her off guard. *Oh, I forgot. I'm black and you're white.*

111

"Sheppy?"

"I'm sorry, Miss M. I was just thinking. Should I read now?"

"A penny for your thoughts."

"It was nothing, really. Winslow and Lena. They both like a lot of the same things. They could be good friends. But . . ."

"Other people won't let them," Miss Montgomery said, her gray eyes flashing. "It's the powerful people. They control things. Money. Laws. Even relationships. They think they know what's best for everybody. But they don't know love. They hurt people and then think they've won something. But they haven't. Love always wins. Always . . ."

Sheppy thought hard for a moment. How did love win if two people couldn't be together? How did love win when a person died?

Miss Montgomery must have been thinking, too, because it was quiet for a while.

"Do you want to continue with the book?" she finally asked. "I think we can finish it today."

Sheppy took her turn, rereading the part she'd missed. Lena's Papa was supposed to be home from fixing Mrs. Chism's fences by Wednesday night, but it was daylight Thursday morning and he still wasn't back. Something was wrong. Lena went looking for him. As she read, Sheppy heard the pounding in her ears get louder. Her heart again. Lena found her father. Hurt. Shot. The pounding. She didn't want to read any more. Didn't want to know. She stopped and held her ears.

"Sheppy, are you all right?"

The pounding slowed. Faded.

' Headache," she said. A lie. But she couldn't explain.

"Why don't we take a rest?"

Sheppy took a deep breath and nodded. Neither of them spoke. Finally Miss Montgomery said, "I know you don't like soap operas, but is there something else on television you'd like to watch?" She handed Sheppy the remote control.

"I like old movies." Sheppy smiled and a tear rolled down her cheek. A tear. She was crying again.

"You mean the kind that make you cry?" Miss Montgomery asked, handing her a tissue.

Sheppy laughed and a wave of tears came crashing down.

"Oh, dear," said Miss Montgomery. "Can I help?"

Sheppy shook her head, "I never read the stuff on the book jacket. I don't like to know what's going to happen. I didn't know about Lena's Papa. He's going to die, too, isn't he?" Her whole body shook. She was sobbing. Out of control.

"My lord, Sheppy, has someone died?"

"Papa," she said, instinctively moving into Miss M's open arms. "My papa."

Chapter
19

"How have things been going at work, honey?" Mama asked. She and Sheppy stood at the kitchen table snapping green beans. "Are you getting along all right with Miss Montgomery?"

Sheppy nodded. "She's nice, Mama. I wasn't sure at first, though."

"Well, everybody takes some getting used to," Mama said.

Sheppy broke the top and bottom ends from a bean, then snapped it in half. *Snip. Snip. Snap.* She liked this chore. She didn't have to think about it. Could think of anything she chose while the restful motion of the task kept the work going. *Snip. Snip. Snap.*

She was tired. Drained. She had told Miss M so much. More than she wanted her to know. About the cancer and the doctors. About Tess and camp. About how everybody in the family had to work harder for money, and how nobody seemed happy anymore.

Sheppy had been relieved when Ranger arrived. But, at the same time, she'd found it hard to leave Miss M.

"How has *your* new job been, Mama?" she asked. She didn't want to talk about herself anymore.

"Just fine. The money isn't bad and your Grandma always said, *hard work keeps you healthy.*"

"Are the people nice?"

Mama didn't answer right away. *Snip. Snip. Snap.* "They're as nice as they know how to be."

As she'd grown up, Sheppy had learned to listen carefully to what her mother said. How she said things. Mama sometimes had a way of saying one thing when she really meant something else.

They're as nice as they know how to be. But how nice did they know how to be? Mama probably meant that they tried to be nice, but it wasn't real. She had said it kindly, as though these were people to pity because they hadn't had much experience with niceness.

Snip. Snip. Snap. Sheppy wished they were nice. Really and truly nice. For Mama's sake.

Suddenly she heard herself say, "Mama, are you doing all right? Without Papa, I mean?"

Snip. Snip. Snap. "I could ask you the same question."

"I'll answer if you will," Sheppy said.

"I don't want you worrying about me, baby. We're all

working on this thing. You just be extra good to yourself right now."

"Mama I . . ."

"I should have gone ahead and let you go to camp," Mama continued. "We'd have managed. You shouldn't have to be spending your vacation this way."

"No, Mama," Sheppy said. She took a step toward her mother and slipped an arm around her waist. "I was upset about camp at first, but it's okay now. I want to be here. With you and Ranger."

They pressed their cheeks together, then, in silence, went back to the rhythm of their work. When they finished, Mama carried the colander to the sink and ran cold water over the beans. Sheppy sat at the table.

"Isn't one of your school friends having a swimming party this week? Wouldn't you like to go?"

Sheppy shrugged.

"And you should be going down to the park some of these afternoons," Mama went on. "Last summer you practically lived there. You need to be spending some time with people your own age. It's not healthy for children to be with grown-ups all the time."

"I don't know, Mama." Sheppy didn't feel much like being with other kids. Not right now. Most everybody was at camp or on vacation anyway.

"Have you written Tessa yet? I'm sure she misses you."

"Not yet," Sheppy confessed. "But I will. Tonight."

"Dinner will be a while. You could do it now."

Mama was trying to get rid of her. She hadn't answered her question about Papa. Yet, she had. Mama *wasn't* all right. How could she be? None of them were.

She went to her room, and took out Papa's tablet.

One of the poems was called "Buttercups and Roses." At the bottom Papa had written, "Dad." Then, "1980." Papa had written it for Grandfather Lee the year he had died. Before she was born. The poem was sad, but not sad at the same time.

Sheppy had never met Grandfather Lee, but she knew him in a way. Papa had told her and Ranger stories about him. Mostly about going to the beach. About how it took Grandfather forever to get ready to go and Grandmother and Papa would get mad. But then, when they finally got to the beach, they wouldn't be mad anymore. Papa always told about crabs and seagulls and being buried in the sand. About the smell of the air by the shore. He even had beach pictures hanging on the walls down in the game room. And the times that Papa took Sheppy and Ranger and Mama to the beach, Mama always teased him about acting like a big kid. He was so happy.

Sheppy looked back over the poem. When his father died, Papa had felt the same pain that Sheppy was feeling now.

She didn't want to think about the pain. She started to close the tablet but couldn't resist flipping the page instead. Though reading the poems made her miss Papa more, it also made her feel closer to him. He was there. In the words. *His* words.

Kiss Me Blue

Love me pretty.
Love me nice.
Love me delicious
with sugar and spice.
Love me with honey
and if that ain't enough,
then love me with chocolates
with almonds and stuff.
Kiss me blue.
Turn me inside out.
That's what loving
is all about.

Sheppy felt giddy. This was Papa. Clever. Playful. Deep with love. He must have really loved Mama.

There was more:

Sleepy time Heaven
with stars falling down.
Soft summer breezes
and leaves swirling 'round.
Living together
in all our dreams.
Filling each moment
with impossible schemes.
Well, shake me silly.
Well, shut my mouth.

That's what loving
is all about.

Some may roam
and others may stray.
Some will linger
or just go away.
Some will be unhappy
for whatever reasons why.
Some live with regret
and let love die.

High as a mountain
Wide as the sun.
There is enough loving
for everyone.
So don't be dismayed
and lock love out.
That's what love
is all about.

Yes, that's what love
is all about.

It was like what Miss M said. Love always wins. Papa
believed it, too.

· · ·

Dear Parker,

   I promised I'd think of something. Well, I don't
know if this will help, but I'm sending you a poem

my father wrote. He said that there's so much love in the world and it's so strong and so wonderful that the bad things can't win. Here it is:

She copied the poem in her best handwriting, then wrote:

Please write me back. I want to know that you're all right. "Don't Be Dismayed and Lock Love Out."

She started to sign it "Your friend" like the earlier letter. Now, somehow, it didn't work for her. Sounded fake. Like part of a letter-writing assignment in school. If she were writing Tess she could say "Love," but she couldn't use that for Parker. "Sincerely" didn't sound sincere.

Sheppy chewed the end of her pen, thinking. Finally she wrote:

Always, Sheppy

．　．　．

She had already dropped the letter into the corner mailbox and let the metal mouth swing back into place when it occurred to her. Was it right to send one of Papa's poems to Parker? She hadn't even shared them with her own family.

Papa had said once, "You'll know in your gut when you're doing something you shouldn't be doing." In third grade, Sheppy had found a five-dollar bill on the playground and told herself it was okay to keep it, even after she'd found out who lost it. Finders keepers. But her stomach didn't stop hurting until she gave the money back. She touched her stomach. It felt fine now. She was trying to help Parker, and that made it right.

She *did* want to show the poems to Mama and Ranger. Soon. As soon as she found the right time. *Timing is important.*

Chapter 20

"You're taking green beans for lunch?" Ranger asked as he drove her to work the next day. He'd seen her put a container of beans, boiled with potatoes and ham, in her bag.

"It's for Miss M," Sheppy said.

"Miss M? It sounds like you two are hitting it off. That's great, but with her money, shouldn't she be giving *you* lunch?"

"She likes Mama's cooking."

Ranger laughed. "I guess I can't blame her for that." He seemed okay today. Maybe things were a little better for him. Or maybe he was becoming a better actor. Still, his eyes seemed distant. Like he was in some other galaxy.

When they pulled into the Montgomerys' driveway there was a white van outside from a place called United Hospital Supplies. What was going on? The front door was open, so Sheppy hurried in.

A man was standing inside waiting for someone to sign a delivery form for a pair of crutches and a wheelchair. Sheppy smiled.

"Yes, Charles. Constance said she called and ordered them," Mrs. Fletcher was saying into the telephone receiver. ". . . I don't know when, but there's someone here who wants an authorization for billing. . . . I think you should just send the things back. She should have discussed this with you." Mrs. Fletcher huffed and looked at her watch. "Well, if that's what you want. I really need to leave. . . . Yes, all right . . . Oh, by the way, another one of those letters came for her . . . Yes . . . Should I leave it where I did the others? . . . Fine. I'll see you then."

She checked her watch again. "Where is that girl?" she asked, turning around. "Oh," she said, catching sight of Sheppy.

Mrs. Fletcher signed the man's paper and closed the door behind him. "I don't know what she expects to be able to do with these," she muttered. "That leg was broken in two places." She looked at Sheppy. "You go on up and see to her. I'll be leaving here in a minute."

As Sheppy turned to go, she saw Mrs. Fletcher pick up an envelope next to the telephone. It was one of those airmail letters, with the red and blue design. *Another one of those letters came for her,* Mrs. Fletcher had told Mr. Montgomery. *Her* had to be Miss Montgomery. Why wouldn't they just give Miss M her mail? Sheppy took her time getting to the steps, hoping to see where she put the letter.

But Mrs. Fletcher turned back toward her and said, "Well, go on."

When Sheppy got upstairs, Miss Montgomery was smiling.

"Did the crutches and wheelchair come?"

"Yes," Sheppy said. "Mrs. Fletcher . . ." She went over to the dumbwaiter, opened the door and listened. When she heard the back door close she continued, "Mrs. Fletcher didn't know what do, so she called Mr. Montgomery. I guess he told her it was okay because she signed for the delivery."

Miss Montgomery clapped her hands together. "Good. I need to get out of this bed."

"Did your doctor say it was all right?"

"He said at some point I should try. I wasn't up to it before, but now I'm feeling ready. Stronger. I wasn't sure whether I could manage crutches, but I'd like to find out. That's why I ordered the chair, too, just in case. You've helped, you know. And your mother's cooking hasn't hurt either."

She smiled at Sheppy, then suddenly she frowned. "Listen to me. I've been thinking only of myself. I haven't even said hello to you." She reached out. "Come here."

Sheppy went over, took her hand, and sat down.

"How are you?"

"Okay," Sheppy said. "I'm sorry about yesterday. It was silly."

"No," Miss Montgomery said. "It wasn't silly. It was important for you to let that happen. You're grieving.

Grief can be extremely destructive unless you can find a way to let go of some of the pain. A healthy way."

She squeezed Sheppy's hand. "What about *Words by Heart*? Would you like to finish it?"

Sheppy did, but she didn't. "Not today," she said and stood up, letting go of Miss Montgomery's hand. "How about lunch?"

"All right. Then will you help me with the crutches?"

"Sure."

· · ·

On the kitchen counter Sheppy found her weekly pay envelope. She glanced inside and saw that there were five twenty-dollar bills. Mr. Montgomery must have made a mistake.

She heated the green beans in the microwave and served them with buttered bread, grapes, and iced tea.

"I've never had beans cooked like this," Miss Montgomery said. "So much flavor."

"It's the ham," Sheppy explained. "Mama says there's no use paying good money for string beans if you don't have enough to buy a nice piece of ham to cook them with."

"She must know what she's talking about."

Speaking of money reminded her. "Miss M, Mr. Montgomery left this week's pay in an envelope downstairs."

"Yes?"

"Well, he paid seventy-five dollars for last week. And, well, today he left me a hundred dollars."

"Yes, I know."

125

"But why?"

"I asked Charles to give you a bit more. You've been bringing food from home, and I've been enjoying it very much. But I can't continue to let you feed me lunch without some compensation."

Sheppy didn't know what to say.

"You'll let me do this for you, won't you?" Miss Montgomery patted Sheppy's arm. "It's not that much, you know."

Sheppy nodded. "Thank you."

"Thank *you*. It's settled then. Now, how about if we tackle those crutches? I need to go to the bathroom."

•   •   •

Miss Montgomery had a hard time at first. The cast covered her leg from hip to toes and seemed to want to drop to the floor as if it were made of lead rather than plaster. She wasn't supposed to put weight on her leg yet, so she had to hold it up away from the floor as she moved herself across the room using the crutches. Sheppy helped her get started, then walked beside and sometimes behind her just in case. They made it to the bathroom, and in a little while, Sheppy helped her up onto the crutches again and they started back. They were only halfway across the room when Miss Montgomery almost lost her balance. Sheppy dragged a chair over and helped her sit on it.

"I think these crutches are too tall. Maybe we should get the wheelchair up here until we figure out how to adjust them. I might need it," Miss Montgomery said, breathing hard. "I'll rest here a bit."

"Okay," Sheppy said and started down the stairs.

"Can you manage it?"

"I don't know. I'll see."

Although the chair was a bit awkward to lift, it was lighter than it appeared and it folded together from side to side. Sheppy held the handles on the back and wheeled it to the stairs. When she passed the telephone stand, she remembered the airmail letter. Should she ask Miss Montgomery about it?

She pulled and bumped the chair up and over each step, letting the big wheels do most of the work. Upstairs she opened the chair and pushed it into the bedroom. Miss Montgomery was back in bed.

"Hey, you made it!" Sheppy said.

"I did, didn't I."

"Should I put this by your bed?"

"That would be fine."

Sheppy sat down. She wanted to tell Miss Montgomery about the letter. But should she? Could she? Mama would probably say it was none of her business. So would Papa. Maybe Mr. Montgomery had his reasons. Maybe whoever was writing her was a bad person, and he was just protecting his niece. Like Ranger would look out for Sheppy.

"I wondered if we could try that game again sometime," Miss Montgomery said.

Sheppy grinned. "Okay! I'll bring the Scrabble board back."

Miss Montgomery handed her the remote control. "But

now, how about one of those old movies you were talking about?"

Sheppy flicked the channels until she saw black-and-white. She recognized the creepy house from *Psycho*. Too scary. She flicked the channel.

"Whew! I'm glad you turned that one off. I've seen it before."

"Me, too. But I had my eyes closed for some parts."

"I can guess which ones."

They laughed and to Sheppy's surprise Miss Montgomery said, "Maybe we should peek back and see what's happening."

She meant to go back, but flicked forward by mistake and stopped when she saw a huge gorilla carrying a woman around the jungle. It was *King Kong*. Fay Wray was screaming her head off. She was the best screamer.

"Oh," Miss Montgomery exclaimed, "I haven't seen this one in years."

"Should we watch?" Sheppy asked, hoping she'd say yes.

She nodded, then shaking her head said, "But it's a sad one, isn't it. That poor creature."

"Do you remember the last line, Miss M?" Sheppy asked.

She thought hard. "Wait, don't tell me." It had come to her. Sheppy could tell by the look on her face.

Just as Miss Montgomery started to speak, Sheppy said it with her: "'Twas beauty killed the beast."

They smiled at each other and settled back to watch,

rooting for King Kong all the way. The time passed quickly and soon King Kong was on the Empire State Building.

"They just should have left him in the jungle. He was happy there," Sheppy said.

"People are always tampering with the lives of others," Miss Montgomery said.

Tampering with the lives of others. The letter. Ranger would be there soon, and she still hadn't told Miss Montgomery about the letter. She wouldn't see her again until Monday. It wasn't right for Mr. Montgomery to be tampering with Miss M's life. If someone was hiding letters from *her,* Sheppy would be mad. Miss Montgomery had a right to know.

"I'm glad Fay has finally fainted. All that screaming," Miss Montgomery said, then studying Sheppy's face asked, "Is there something on your mind?"

She would tell her. She had to. "Yes, ma'am. I mean, Miss M. I was just wondering, do you know somebody in another country?"

The look of pleasure faded from Miss Montgomery's face. She seemed to go pale. She picked up the remote control and turned off the sound on the TV.

Then, as if afraid of something, she said, "Why? Why do you ask that?"

"A letter came. In an airmail envelope. I think it was for you. I heard Mrs. Fletcher tell Mr. Montgomery on the phone. She put it away somewhere, I think. And . . ."

Sheppy was stopped by a cry that made her jump in her chair. A cry of anger. Of pain. Miss Montgomery. Her gray stare cut to Sheppy. She took a deep breath, then let it out and asked, "And what?"

Sheppy was afraid to say more but knew she had to finish what she'd started. "Um. Well, it sounded like there were more letters, because Mrs. Fletcher asked if she should put the one that came today with the others."

"Where! Where did she put them?" Miss Montgomery demanded. "Get them for me. Please."

"I didn't see, Miss M. I'm sorry."

She heard the door open downstairs. Mrs. Fletcher.

They looked at each other. Sheppy couldn't get the letters now.

"I'm sorry," she said again.

Miss Montgomery took Sheppy's hand and pulled her closer.

"Can you come tomorrow?" she whispered, her eyes wet.

"I . . . I don't know."

"Uncle Charles plays golf every Saturday morning." Miss Montgomery spoke quickly and quietly. "He leaves at seven. That Fletcher woman comes over, but not until eight. I'll be alone." She was squeezing Sheppy's hand so hard it hurt. "Can you come then?"

"Maybe." Sheppy thought fast. She wanted to help, but she wasn't sure. Miss Montgomery was scaring her. "I don't know how I'd get here. And how would I get in?" Excuses. She was finding excuses.

"My uncle keeps a key to the back door under one of

the rocks surrounding the back flower bed, the rock farthest from the door, I think."

Beep! Ranger was there.

Miss Montgomery held Sheppy's hand tighter. "Please come. I need you to find those letters."

"Maybe I shouldn't ask, but who do you think they're from?"

Miss Montgomery sighed and looked toward the window. "He's my . . . I guess you could call him my Winslow."

Sheppy's heart started to pound. "Maybe I could ride my bike."

Chapter

21

As they drove home, Sheppy wanted to tell Ranger about her plans to go back to the Montgomerys' on Saturday, but she couldn't. Couldn't tell Mama either. She knew they wouldn't let her go. Wouldn't want her to get in the middle of whatever problem Miss M was having with her uncle. But Sheppy *was* going.

Ranger was quiet. It hurt her to look at his eyes. Would he be forever changed? Would she never again see the Ranger she'd grown up with? The Ranger who had always made her feel safe?

She leaned her head back on the seat and remembered another set of eyes. Miss Montgomery's.

My Winslow, she had said. Sheppy'd known what Miss M meant right away. When they were reading about Winslow and Lena in *Words by Heart,* Miss M had said that powerful people think they know what's best for everybody. Mr. Montgomery must be keeping her away from a close friend. Maybe even someone she was in love with. It must be why she seemed unhappy.

Still she'd said *love always wins.* How could she believe that if she and her friend weren't together? And how long had they been apart? A month? A year? Ten years? After ten years, how could a person still believe? It was like something out of a movie. A wonderful and terrible movie. And now Sheppy had a part in it, too. Maybe she could help the story have a happy ending.

"I've got to go," Ranger said, stopping the car in front of the house. He touched her hair as she got out. "You have your key?"

Sheppy reached in her purse and held the key ring up for him to see.

As he drove away she waved, feeling his sadness. She wished William and Roland would come back. Or that Ranger would find a new girlfriend. Or get back together with Hayley. They'd seemed so great together.

Sheppy wondered why they had broken up. It happened after Papa got sick. How could Hayley pick such a lousy time to leave? But maybe she hadn't wanted to go. Maybe Ranger had shut her out, like he was doing to Sheppy now.

Before going into the house, she went to the mailbox. Maybe there was something from Parker. There was a sweepstakes entry and something from the hospital, probably a bill. Sheppy felt good to have some money to give to Mama. *And* there was a letter from Tess.

· · ·

Upstairs, Sheppy ripped open the envelope and fell across her bed.

Dear Sheppy,

Is everything okay? When I didn't get a letter the first few days I figured you were just busy or waiting to have some news about your job. Now I think it's something else. It's weird not knowing what you're thinking. Camp isn't the same without you. But being away has made me think about things. I guess I was trying to act like nothing has changed. But that was dumb. Your papa died. I'm supposed to be your best friend and you couldn't talk to me about it. I've figured out that it was my fault. I'm sorry. I miss you.

Love always and <u>forever,</u>
Tess

P.S. I saw Roberta stuffing Kleenex in her bra this morning. HA! Her bra may be real, but . . .

"Forever" was underlined three times. Sheppy laughed and hugged the letter to her chest. She hoped she could find Miss Montgomery's letters in the morning, and that they would make her feel this good.

• • •

Dear Tessy,

I wanted to write, but I guess I didn't know what to say. I was feeling a lot of different things. I was— am—missing you, but felt kind of bad because it sounded like you were having a good time without me. I thought maybe since you'd found Roberta, you didn't miss me. I'm sorry that I didn't just write and tell you that.

It hasn't been all your fault. It's been hard for me to talk to Ranger and Mama, too. We talk about everyday things. But not about important things. Like Papa. Everybody's so sad. I hope you understand, but I have to say I'm glad that I didn't come to camp. I need to be here.

I have a lot to tell you about my job and about Miss Montgomery. A LOT! But not in a letter. I'll tell you when you come home.

I hope the rest of camp is good. I mean it. I want you to have a good time, even without me. Call me again if you can. I miss you.

Love always and <u>forever,</u>

Sheppy

P.S. I got a letter from Parker Ford. Things aren't too good for him and his family. I've written him back. He's not a lizard at all, Tess. I thought you should know that I think we're becoming friends.

Sheppy went up to bed early. She told Mama she was reading a new book, and she was. *Jackaroo* was just what she needed. It was about lords and ladies and a legendary hero like Robin Hood. It took place in a far-off land in the distant past, a place Sheppy was happy to go. There was even a map in the front. *Thank you, Cynthia Voigt.* At ten o'clock she wanted to keep reading but turned out the light, remembering her plans for the morning.

She closed her eyes and imagined herself as Jackaroo riding gallantly up to Miss M's house, unsheathing her sword and demanding that Mr. Montgomery turn over the letters. Then suddenly Papa was there. No, he wasn't there. But she could hear him. Not his voice. His music.

Sheppy sat up in bed and listened. "Rhapsody in Blue." She thought she must be dreaming, but knew she was awake. She got out of bed and ran to her door, her heart pounding. She stopped and listened again. The music continued, but something was different. The timing. And . . . there, she heard it again. A missed note.

She tiptoed into the hall, sat at the top of the stairs, and looked through the banister. Ranger. It was Ranger. She had never heard him play "Rhapsody." He must have been working on it when she wasn't at home.

Suddenly he stopped. He'd made another mistake. Sheppy thought he would just bang the keys, but he started playing again, repeating the part where he'd made the mistake. He wanted to get it right. If Papa were there he would have played the part for Ranger to show him how it goes, and they would have taken turns playing it over and over again twenty times or more until Ranger'd finally smile and say, "Yeah, I got it. I got it." Nodding his head to the rhythm of the music.

Ranger was playing again. Really playing. Sheppy wanted to go downstairs and tell her brother how proud she was of him. To thank him for learning "Rhapsody in

Blue." But she knew it would be like walking in on a private conversation. Between Ranger and Papa.

· · ·

Back in her room, the moon cast a dim light through her window. It was a thin crescent tonight. The promise that a full moon would return. Sheppy jumped into bed and let the rhapsody enter her dreams.

Chapter 22

She had pushed the snooze alarm twice before getting up, but at 6:30 the next morning, Sheppy was on her way. Ranger was still asleep when she left, so she didn't have to explain anything to him. But Mama was getting ready to go open the Laundromat.

"Where are you off to at this hour?" she had asked.

"I feel like I haven't gotten any exercise lately," Sheppy lied. "And it's too hot to ride in the afternoon."

"Well," Mama'd said, "it's good to see you getting out."

Sheppy smiled to herself remembering how pleased and surprised Mama had been when she'd given her the hundred dollars. After Sheppy explained about the extra money, Mama gave her twenty-five dollars back, saying she had counted on only seventy-five.

"You've earned this extra money by doing an extra fine

job. Doing more than Miss Montgomery asked of you."
Mama hugged her and whispered in her ear, "He would be
so proud."

He was Papa. She was talking about him. Maybe things
were getting better.

Sheppy pumped her legs hard on the upgrade, keeping
the syllables of the words in her head in time with her
pedaling. MAY-BE-THINGS-ARE-GET-TING-BET-
TER.

Just as Sheppy arrived, Mr. Montgomery was coming
out of the house. Quickly she got off her bike and hid
between some bushes and the stone wall at the front of the
property. Mr. Montgomery opened the garage door, then
the trunk of his car. He went into the garage and then came
back around and put his golf clubs in the trunk. Sheppy
checked her watch. 7:07. It was getting late. When Mr.
Montgomery finally drove away, she leaned her bike
against the wall where Mrs. Fletcher wouldn't see it, and
ran around back.

The rock farthest from the door. She picked it up. There
was the key. She giggled, partly from nervousness, partly
because she suddenly saw herself in a drama of suspense and
romance. Mary Sheppard Lee—Code name: Germ—Oc-
cupation: Secret Agent—Mission: Locate stolen letters.

Sheppy let herself into the house.

"Sheppy?" Miss Montgomery called.

"Yes, I'm here," she yelled back, running up the stairs.

Miss Montgomery was sitting on the side of the bed
bracing herself with the crutches.

"You made it! Did you ride your bike?"

Sheppy nodded, a little breathless, and asked, "Where do you think I should start?"

Miss Montgomery looked concerned. "Why don't you rest a minute first."

"I'm okay," Sheppy said. "I don't want to waste time. You said Mrs. Fletcher would be here by eight, and we're burnin' daylight." She'd heard John Wayne say that in one of his westerns.

Miss Montgomery laughed. "I suppose you're right. Well, they must be downstairs since Fletcher didn't come up here to put away the letter that came yesterday. Try some of the bureau drawers down there."

"Okay," Sheppy said and ran back downstairs. She found linen tablecloths and napkins, silverware, photographs, a stamp collection, cassettes, but no letters. She found a bunch of envelopes, but they were old bills and legal papers.

"Sheppy?" Miss Montgomery again.

Sheppy opened the dumbwaiter door and called upstairs, "Nothing yet, Miss M."

She walked to the middle of the living room and stood there. The wheels were spinning in her head. She walked to the bottom of the stairs and called, "Miss M?"

"Yes? Did you find them?"

"No, not yet. Is there a safe in the house?" That was where the important stuff usually was in the movies.

It was quiet, then Miss Montgomery called back. "I don't think so. But Uncle Charles does have a desk that he

140

keeps locked. It's in that space off the living room. I don't know where he keeps the key, though."

Sheppy thought a moment. Where do people usually keep the desk key? "I'll go see," she said, turning toward the living room.

The desk was a beautiful antique, all polished and uncluttered. Sheppy carefully opened, searched and closed all the drawers, except one. The one that was locked. Key. Where would he put the key?

Sheppy checked her watch. 7:40. She was running out of time. Mr. Montgomery had hidden the back door key under a rock. *Under* something. She lifted the lamp on the desk. Nothing. She lifted the blotter. No. Under the rock *farthest away*. Sheppy looked around the small space. There was a table in a corner with a statue on it. It was that blindfolded woman holding the scales. The one that's supposed to stand for justice. Sheppy ran over and carefully moved it to the side. A tiny key reflected the sunlight coming in through the window.

She took it to the drawer and slipped it into the lock. Turn. *Click*. It opened. And there were the letters. Two neat little stacks of them. Maybe fifteen in each held together with rubber bands. She flipped through them with her thumb. All were from T. Bey in Marrakesh, Morocco, and addressed to Mrs. Constance M. Bey. Bey? Was Miss M married?

When Sheppy took the stack from the drawer, there was an empty space where they had been. If she'd been a real secret agent, she'd have come prepared. She'd have made up some fake letters to put in place of the real ones so Mr. Montgomery wouldn't notice they were missing. But it was too late for that now. She shuffled some things around in the drawer to fill the gap before locking it, then returned the key to its hiding place under Justice.

Miss Montgomery was in the wheelchair when Sheppy got upstairs. "I found them, Miss M."

"Bless you," she said, her eyes anxiously scanning the front of the top envelope. She ran her hands over the stacks of letters. "Bless you. You can't know what this means to me."

But Sheppy wanted to know. "Miss M," she asked, "were you married to him?"

Miss Montgomery hesitated, looking at the letters. Sheppy could tell she wanted to read them. "I suppose I owe you some explanation." She laid the letters in her lap, wheeled the chair over to window, and looked out.

"We met in college. I was twenty-four. I attended right after my mother died of leukemia. We were always close, but she became my whole world after my father's death. He and Uncle Charles were swimming in the river and my uncle got caught in the current. Father had a heart attack saving his life. I was sixteen. That's when Mother turned all of our affairs over to Uncle Charles. The house, the money, everything. She put him in charge of a trust fund for me until I'm thirty, believing that I wasn't capable. And I probably wasn't. I had never really done anything. Never had a job. I was one of those well-off kids who took things for granted. That's why I went to college. I needed to find a life.

"And, yes, Turie and I were married. Still are legally, but the real marriage lasted only two weeks. Turie is from Morocco and Uncle Charles got it into his head that he only wanted to marry me to get United States citizenship. And to get my money. My uncle knows important people, and he's a good lawyer. He found out that Turie had a temporary visa permitting him to be in this country only to study, and my uncle managed to keep it from being renewed. Turie had to return to Morocco. And Uncle Charles has been trying to have the marriage annulled ever since."

"But how could you let him? Why didn't you go to Morocco with Turie?"

"By the time I realized what was happening, it was all over. I was never a strong person. I'd never had to fight for anything in my life, and now that I had something to fight for, I didn't know how. It didn't help that Uncle Charles had everyone convinced that I was incapable of handling my own affairs. And I guess I began to think so, too. Especially afterwards."

"Why? What happened then?"

"Before he left, Turie called me from the airport. He promised to write to me, to send for me. He said we would find a way. So I waited, but I never heard from him. My uncle said it proved he was right about him. That Turie never really cared for me." Her voice sounded shaky. "But he *did* care," she whispered, pressing the stack of letters to

143

her breast. Then her voice got loud, angry. "How could Uncle Charles keep them from me?"

"When did this happen?" Sheppy asked.

"About a year and half ago," Miss Montgomery said, her eyes full.

"But what did you *do* after that?" Sheppy was sorry to be asking so many questions, but she couldn't help it.

Miss Montgomery sighed. "I didn't take very good care of myself. Oh!" she said, suddenly wheeling away from the window, "Fletcher's coming. Sheppy, she can't find you here. She tells my uncle everything." She wheeled over to the bed and slipped the letters into a drawer in the night table.

She heard the back door open. Quickly Sheppy looked around for a way out. Under the bed? She could hear the click of high heels on the kitchen floor. In the closet? Was Mrs. Fletcher coming up the stairs?

Then her eyes stopped at the door to the dumbwaiter. It was a wild idea, but there wasn't time to come up with another.

She ran over and opened the door. Could she fit? It was tight, but yes. She managed to squeeze inside. Miss Montgomery wheeled over and whispered, "I'll try to get her upstairs and keep her here until you're down and out."

"Okay. But won't she hear the dumbwaiter going?"

"The motor is pretty quiet, but I'll make sure she doesn't. Then I'll send you down," Miss Montgomery said. She started to close the door but stopped for a second and said, "Thank you, Sheppy. Thank you." Then she asked, "Are you all right in there?"

"I think so."

Miss Montgomery patted Sheppy's hand and closed the door. Then Sheppy heard her wheel the chair away, and the television came on at high volume. Miss Montgomery wheeled the chair back to the dumbwaiter and started ringing her bell loudly. Sheppy heard Mrs. Fletcher yelling something and coming up the stairs.

The dumbwaiter started to move. It was hot in there and dark. Scary, but fun. Still Sheppy was glad when the platform stopped. She had begun to imagine what might happen if she got stuck. She pushed open the door with her feet, slipped out, and tiptoed out the back door.

She started toward her bike, and then, like a good secret agent, she remembered to go back and put the door key under the farthest rock.

Sheppy got on her bike and headed home. Mission accomplished. Letters found. Sooner or later Mr. Montgomery would discover they were missing. What would happen then? Would Sheppy lose her job?

She couldn't think about that now. She just let herself enjoy the lightness of heart she was feeling. Coasting downhill through the cool wind, she thought back to her *narrow* escape in the dumbwaiter and laughed at her own pun. What a ride!

Chapter 23

Sheppy sailed around the corner and onto their street. A police car was parked in front of her house. She hit the brakes. A police car? Had Mrs. Fletcher found out already and turned her in? She jumped off her bike, letting it fall to the ground, and ran inside.

Ranger, Mama, and two officers were sitting in the living room talking. She heard the word "burglary." Still in his bathrobe, Ranger looked up and, when he saw her, made a face like he was in physical pain.

"Excuse me," Mama said to the officers. She came over, squeezed Sheppy's hand, and walked her into the kitchen.

"What's going on, Mama? Why are they here? Is Ranger in trouble?"

"It's okay, honey," she said, but didn't look like she believed it. "I'll talk to you about it after they've gone. Right now I need you to go on up to your room."

"Is Ranger going to jail?"

"No, Ranger is *not* going to jail." Mama hugged Sheppy and turned her toward the doorway. "Now go on. I'll be up later."

．　．　．

When Sheppy got to her bedroom, she left the door open and stood there listening. She could still hear talking but couldn't make out what anyone was saying. Finally she gave up and lay on the bed, hugging her pillow.

Mama had said that Ranger wasn't going to jail. Sheppy wanted to believe it. Just like she'd wanted to believe that Papa wasn't going to die. Wanted to believe in the possibles. *Anything can happen, child. Anything can be.* But Papa was gone. And now . . . Oh, please, don't let them take Ranger away.

She pulled herself up onto her knees and put the top of her head down on the bed. She felt better this way. Upside down.

She closed her eyes and punched her fists into the bed. Mad. Mad at Ranger. How could he do this? Never took an apple from Cook's trees. Mad at Mama. Couldn't she see that things weren't right with Ranger? Sheppy had seen. Why hadn't she? Mad at Papa. This would never have happened if he were here. Why hadn't he become a pianist or something where there weren't any chemicals? Mad at God. Why was He so mean? So mean. Mad. Mad. Mad.

Then there were arms around her. Mama?

"Shep?"

No. Ranger.

He pulled her closer, and she hit him, crying, "You said it would be okay. You said you could handle things."

"Please, Sheppy, please, I'm sorry," he said, still holding on to her.

"No, no," she said, fighting him, "I want Papa!"

Ranger let her fall back onto the bed and said softly, "So do I." Then he put his face in his hands and sobbed.

"Oh, Range," Sheppy said. "Range." And finally they held tight to each other and cried. Cried until they'd let go of all they needed to.

Sheppy pulled some tissues from a box by her bed and handed the box to Ranger.

He blew his nose and said, "Mama was going to come up, but I wanted to be the one to tell you."

"What, Range?" She didn't want to know.

"There was another burglary in Beacon Heights last night."

Sheppy frowned, confused. "But you were home last night. I heard you playing the piano. Papa's song. You weren't even there. I'll tell them."

"No, I wasn't there. I wasn't at the other place either. But I helped them, Sheppy." He couldn't look her in the eyes. "The police were questioning everybody who works for the people who were robbed. When they showed up today, I told them everything."

"I don't understand."

"When I cut lawns, sometimes I could find out when

the people who lived there were going to be away. I didn't ask, but I'd overhear things. Or sometimes they'd tell me they needed the lawn done before they went out of town on a particular day."

Sheppy's stomach ached. "You told the burglars, didn't you?"

"Yes, I . . ."

"But why, Range? You're not like that. You're not!"

Ranger sighed. "I never thought I was, Sheppy. And when these guys first came to me, I said no. They said they'd pay me. More than I could make doing lawns all summer. I still didn't go for it. But they kept after me. They pushed me around and smashed the car headlight. And I couldn't stop thinking about the money."

"But with my job and yours and Mama's, we were doing okay."

"Do you call Mama having to scrub some white man's floor doing okay?"

It was Mr. Hyde again. Ranger never used to talk about white people like they were the enemy. Those burglar jerks had him all twisted around.

He walked over to the desk and sat down facing the wall. "I couldn't stand it, Sheppy. I hate what she has to do. I hear her crying at night sometimes. I hate it!" He got quiet.

Mama crying at night. Like Parker's dad.

Sheppy remembered how she'd felt when Mama told her about the people she worked for. *Nice as they know how to be.* She had wished things were different for Mama but didn't think there was anything she could do about it. Ranger had tried to do something. The wrong thing. But, at least, something.

"And, Papa," Ranger continued, calmer now. "Right before . . . He said I'm the man of the family now, that I should take care of you and Mama. What would he think of me?" He was crying again. Not sobbing. Tears just rolled down his cheeks in silence.

Sheppy went over and put her arms around his neck from behind. "Papa would *love* you, Range, just like he always did. No matter what. And *I* love you." She kissed both his cheeks and said, "Love you, love you, madly."

Ranger smiled and said, "That sounds like something Papa used to say."

Sheppy nodded. Knew it was time. She opened her desk drawer and pulled out the tablet. "I have something to show you."

Chapter 24

Sheppy felt the familiar band of heat across her face. Sun. Her eyes felt puffy. What had happened? Was it still Saturday? After she had showed Ranger the tablet, he'd asked if he could take it to his room. "I'd like some time alone," he'd said.

Sheppy wasn't sure whether the poems would make him feel better or worse. After he left she'd dropped on her bed, tired from the morning. Must have fallen asleep. She looked at her watch. Still only eleven o'clock.

She rolled over and wrinkled her nose. She needed a shower. On her way to the bathroom she thought of checking on Ranger, but his door was closed. Not now.

In the shower Sheppy closed her eyes and held her face under the water. The steamy spray felt good. So good that, for a minute, she could imagine it might wash away all the things that weren't right.

She still didn't know what was going to happen to Ranger. He had committed a crime. And she might be in trouble herself for getting those letters. She could get fired. And maybe that wasn't the worst thing that could happen. If Mr. Montgomery was a good enough lawyer to get somebody thrown out of the country, wouldn't it be easy for him to have Sheppy arrested?

She was worried about Mama, too. Was she all right? She'd been crying at night, Ranger had said. Was that good or bad? If only you could see a person on the inside.

· · ·

Sheppy found her mother ironing in the living room. Mama's favorite radio station was on—WJAZ. The station played only jazz. Sometimes she'd hear Mama listening at night. Sheppy recognized the song that was playing— "Stormy Weather." Lena Horne was singing. Sheppy wished Mama were singing along like she used to. She wasn't.

"Hi, baby," Mama said. She looked exhausted.

"Is there stuff I can iron?" Sheppy asked, looking through a basket of clean laundry. She wasn't very good at doing dresses or shirts with collars, but she could iron tee shirts and shorts, sheets, and pillowcases. There were some.

"Let me iron for a while, Mama. Why don't you take a rest?"

Mama looked up and smiled. Then she set the iron upright, turned it off, and came over and hugged Sheppy.

"Are you all right?" they said at the same time.

Together they laughed, then Mama walked her over to the couch and they sat down.

"Did Ranger explain what happened?"

"Yes, Mama. What will happen to him now?"

"When he's ready, I'll take him to the police station to make a statement. That's all that'll happen today. In a few weeks, there will be a hearing, a kind of meeting, in juvenile court. Until then, they'll be leaving him in my custody. That means I'm responsible for making sure he stays out of trouble and attends the hearing. The officers today said that since this was Ranger's first offense and he's cooperating with them, they would recommend probation."

Sheppy frowned. What did that mean? The question must have shown in her face.

"Ranger won't have to go to jail, but he'll have his freedom on a trial basis. On a promise of good behavior. And they'll be keeping a close watch on him for a period of time."

Ranger wasn't going away. Sheppy let out a breath, relaxed a little. Then she thought of something.

"Mama, you said Ranger was cooperating with the police. Does that mean he confessed, or that he's telling the police who the burglars are?"

"Both," Mama said.

Her stomach felt tight again. She was remembering the car headlight. "But Mama, those guys could hurt Ranger. Does he have to tell?"

"They won't be able to hurt him if they're in prison."

But what about when they got out? It had happened in that movie, *Cape Fear*. Robert Mitchum came back from prison and tried to kill Gregory Peck and his whole family. She closed her eyes, trying to block it out of her mind. Why had she even watched it?

"Sheppy, it's going to be all right. Your brother did a bad thing, but now he's doing a good thing. Sometimes doing the right thing means sacrificing something. Or taking a risk. Ranger knows that. He's a good person. He'll come through this. We all will."

Sheppy laid her head on Mama's lap. "He is a good person, Mama. He *is.*"

Mama patted Sheppy's shoulder. "He just got things all mixed up. Something your papa said has been tearing him up inside."

She paused. Then went on, "I don't think your father knew how much you kids needed his approval on everything. He had high ideals and expectations, and wanted you to have them, too. But Ranger is still only seventeen; he's just a boy. Your papa made him think he had to take on the responsibilities of a man."

Sheppy sat up. It bothered her, the way Mama was talking. Like she was blaming Papa for what Ranger had done. Like she was mad at him. After all the nice things Papa had said about her in his poems. Then as quickly as Sheppy had drawn away, she lay back down and pulled Mama's arm around her, remembering. She had been mad at Papa, too. Just this morning. She had been mad at him.

Billie Holiday was singing on the radio. Mama squeezed Sheppy's hand and sang along. Sheppy's wish had come true. But the sadness in her mother's voice made her wish it hadn't. Sheppy's heart ached. It must have been what Ranger felt. What had driven him to be something he wasn't.

"Mama, is there anything I can do to help?"

She stopped singing. "Baby, you're already doing something. You're here, sitting with me now. You're helping around the house. And you're earning money for the family when you should be away at camp enjoying your summer vacation. The truth is, it's time for me to start being a real mother to you kids again."

She smoothed Sheppy's hair back and went on. "I *am* grateful for your job, though. Especially now that Ranger has most likely lost his."

Sheppy sucked in her breath. Ranger lost his job. It made sense. But what if she lost hers, too? Her head swam. She closed her eyes and forced herself to think of nothing. Blank white paper. White paper. White paper.

• • •

Sheppy was finishing her part of the ironing when Ranger came downstairs, freshly showered and dressed. Clean. He seemed tired, but the distant look he had been carrying in his eyes was gone.

He came over and hugged her, lifting her feet off the floor like old times.

"Thanks for this morning," he said.

She smiled at him. The poems. Maybe they had helped.

Mama came in from the kitchen and studied Ranger. Checking to see if he was all right.

He kissed her cheek. "I'm ready to get this statement over with," he said.

Mama nodded. "I thought maybe we could do something together tonight," she said. "Go to a show and have a bite to eat. How about it?"

"I'd like that," Ranger said. "Why don't you check the movie listings while we're gone, Shep?"

She wanted to, but then she wondered about the money.

"We could just rent something and order pizza," Sheppy said. "I could pop popcorn, too."

Ranger laughed. "Oh, I forgot. It's hard to find a black-and-white movie at the theater. I'm up for it. How about you, Mama?"

"Fine," she said, checking her purse for the car keys. "Maybe I'll make some cookies."

"Peanut butter?" Sheppy asked.

"Are there any other kind?"

"Hey, what about a game of Monopoly after the movie?" Ranger said, rubbing his hands together.

"Or Scrabble," Mama said.

"No way!" Sheppy said.

Ranger put his arm around Mama's shoulder and squeezed her next to him. "You always win."

Sheppy walked them to the door.

"Decide what you want to see and I'll take you to the

156

video place when we get back," Ranger said, squeezing her hand.

Sheppy waved as they drove away, trying not to think about where they were going. She focused on tonight. What movie did she want to see? Something that would make them feel good. Something with a happy ending. *It's a Wonderful Life.*

Chapter
25

Sheppy wasn't listening to Reverend Callaway's sermon. She tried, but her mind kept wandering. She was remembering how mad she had been at God the day before. How she'd punched her bed. Had she been punching God in her heart? She prayed for forgiveness. Sheppy didn't want Him to be mad at her, especially today. She needed to ask something.

Please, God. I'm sorry about yesterday. I was scared about Ranger. Sometimes it seems like you don't care. I try to believe you do. I still don't understand why you took Papa from us. But now that you have, please take care of us. Don't let Mr. Montgomery fire me. For Mama's sake. And Ranger's. Maybe I shouldn't have gotten the letters for Miss Montgomery. It's hard to know what's right anymore.

Ranger nudged her. The rest of the church was standing, singing,

> *What a fellowship, what a joy divine,*
> *leaning on the everlasting arms.*

She jumped up and joined in, hoping Mama didn't see her from the choir loft. Sheppy checked her mother's face. No. She was deep within the music.

> *What a blessedness, what a peace is mine,*
> *leaning on the everlasting arms.*

Singing helped Mama. Standing with the choir, she always had a look of joy. Peace. Sheppy wished Mama could keep that forever.

Sheppy had been attending Sunday school and church services at Calvary A.M.E. church for as long as she could remember and had never felt the spirit of the Lord like everybody talked about. She'd wanted to. Had tried to. Once, when Sheppy was little, she'd held on to the Reverend's robe as he passed by the pew, thinking maybe she could feel it through him, but nothing happened. Except the Reverend almost tripped and Papa gave her a piece of his mind and made her apologize to the Reverend later. She had listened hard to sermons and concentrated on the good feeling. Nothing. She had focused her eyes on the big cross on the wall behind the pulpit and prayed for the feeling. Nothing.

Sometimes she had pretended to feel it. And she'd probably fooled some people, but she knew it wasn't real. And God knew.

She'd watched Mama sing many times. But, this morning, it was different. The glow about Mama seemed to fill the room and soak right through Sheppy's skin. And Sheppy was overwhelmed with something. Something deep.

> *Leaning*
> *Leaning*
> *Safe and secure from all alarms*
> *Leaning*
> *Leaning*
> *Leaning on the everlasting arms.*

Chapter

26

"Sheppy, why aren't you up? You need to get ready for work," Mama said, shaking her awake.

But she was already awake. Concentrating. Trying to recapture the safe feeling of the day before.

"I think I'm sick, Mama," she said, sounding as sick as she could.

"What is it, baby?" Mama was sympathetic. Good.

"My stomach," Sheppy said, which wasn't really a lie. Her stomach did hurt, but not because she was sick. It was a different kind of hurt. The kind she felt when she'd done something bad enough to get a licking. Or when it was her turn to go on stage during a play. Or when she'd found that five-dollar bill.

Mama felt Sheppy's forehead. "You don't have a fever. What did you eat last night?"

"Just dinner and some cookies later."

"How many cookies?"

"Two," Sheppy lied. Then she confessed, "No, four." She didn't want to make things any worse. Even a little bit.

"Well," Mama said, "sometimes it's hard to tell how you feel until you get up and move around. I'll get you some Pepto, and then you go on and take your shower."

Pepto Bismol. Yuck. "Can I take my shower first? Then if I feel better, I won't need the medicine. Don't people say that if you take medicine when you don't need it, it won't work when you do need it?"

Mama smiled. "All right, go on."

• • •

Ranger had to meet with a social worker from the court, so Mama drove Sheppy to work.

On the way, Mama asked, "Sheppy, is there some reason you don't want to go to the Montgomerys'? Has something happened there to upset you?"

Sheppy didn't want to lie anymore, but didn't want to worry Mama either. It was easier to hide a thing when nobody asked. Like what Lena did with Mrs. Chism's books in *Words by Heart*. But it was still a lie. It was right that she tell Mama. But there was too much to tell, and already they were turning into the Montgomerys' driveway.

Mama stopped the car. "Sheppy?"

"Mama," she said quickly, "there *may* be something. But I can't tell you now." She took off her seat belt.

Mama studied Sheppy's face. Sheppy tried to look calm and confident.

Mama turned off the engine. "I'll come in with you today. Just to say hello."

For a moment, Sheppy couldn't breathe. "No, Mama, please," she managed to say. Then she took a breath and went on, "You always say, 'Try to finish what you start, even if you feel like turning and running in the other direction.' I want to try. On my own, Mama. I promise I'll tell you later."

Mama reached over and held Sheppy's chin in her hand. She looked at Sheppy's face a moment, then she turned the ignition key and started the engine.

"Thanks," Sheppy said, getting out. She closed the car door and peeked back in. "Mama?" She wanted to say something more. Thanks didn't seem to be enough.

"Yes?"

"I . . ." She ran around the car and hugged her through the window. "I'll see you later."

"If Harvey didn't know these people, I wouldn't be doing this," Mama said, shifting the car into gear.

Sheppy waved until the car was out of sight. She knew what she was doing. Avoiding going in. But maybe there was nothing to worry about.

Sheppy rang the doorbell and Mrs. Fletcher answered as always. She never looked friendly, but today her expression seemed worse than usual.

Her face was red and puffy. A lock of her hair, which normally was sprayed neatly in place, fell across her cheek. She pushed it back behind her ear, saying, "Mr. Montgomery wants to see you in his study."

Mr. Montgomery? What was he doing home? Sheppy's stomach turned over.

Mrs. Fletcher picked up her purse and a big shopping bag and clicked past Sheppy out the front door. The woman's slip was hanging below the hem of the flowered dress she wore. Mrs. Fletcher would want to know, and Sheppy was surprised to find herself resisting an urge to run and tell her. To save her embarrassment.

Sheppy closed the front door and walked to the study.

"Mary, come in, please. And sit down." Mr. Montgomery was being very polite, but Sheppy could hear the edge in his voice. He was sitting behind his desk when she went in. The desk that she had broken into just two days before. She sat down in the chair facing the desk. Already her underarms were damp.

He leaned back in his chair and stared at her. Like he was trying to figure something out. Finally he said, "I would prefer to discuss this with your mother, but Constance . . ." He cleared his throat and went on.

"In the short time you've worked in this house you've managed to accomplish a great deal. You've formed an intimate relationship with my niece through which you've learned family secrets, you've invaded the privacy of my desk, eliminated Mrs. Fletcher . . ."

Mrs. Fletcher? What . . . ?

". . . *and* finagled a raise, I might add. Cleverness is a quality I admire. However, you were not hired to be clever. You were hired to follow my instructions."

But what about Miss M's instructions?

164

"I no longer want you in this house," he went on.

There it is. She looked at her hands folded in her lap. They started to blur as her eyes filled up. She wanted to stay. And, just then, realized it wasn't because of the money, but because of Miss M. Sheppy wanted to read more books with her and watch more movies and maybe even a soap opera. She wanted to play Scrabble with her again like Miss M said. She wanted to help her get better and to find out if she would have a happy ending with the man from Morocco.

"My wish is to terminate you today." He shuffled some papers on his desk. "But *Constance* wants you here."

Sheppy looked up, surprised. *She* told *him* she wants me here?

Mr. Montgomery's voice softened. He looked past Sheppy as if he were talking to someone else. "And I suppose I've made decisions for her too often in the past. She always seemed to need someone to take care of her. And she was my responsibility after my brother . . ." Suddenly he focused on Sheppy again.

"You were wrong to involve yourself in matters that don't concern you."

"Yes, sir," Sheppy said.

He cleared his throat. "My niece seems to have improved in the time you've been here." He leaned forward in his chair. "Tell me," he said. "What's your secret?" There was a slight smile on his face, but a sadness, too. Sheppy could tell he wanted to be closer to Miss M.

She shrugged. She didn't know how to answer. "I just tried to be friends with her."

Mr. Montgomery looked down and nodded. "We'll be keeping you on for two more weeks. Constance will explain."

Two weeks? Sheppy felt her stomachache coming back. She *was* being fired.

Chapter

27

Sheppy's whole body felt heavy as she went upstairs. Mr. Montgomery had left the house after his lecture, and she was to stay with Miss Montgomery as usual. But only for two more weeks. What would happen after that?

"Sheppy, dear," Miss Montgomery said, motioning her to sit on the bed. "You've been talking with my uncle?"

Sheppy nodded and sat down.

"I don't want to go, Miss M," she said, fighting back tears. She tried not to whine.

"What did he tell you?"

"That I have to leave in two weeks, and that I *eliminated* Mrs. Fletcher somehow. I don't understand."

"You had nothing to do with that woman's departure," Miss Montgomery said, anger in her voice. "She and I had words after you left on Saturday. Uncle Charles has no right to blame you. It was all my doing, and I'm glad of it. So don't blame yourself."

She patted Sheppy's knee and continued, "She never liked me. Never wanted to help really. She has a thing for Uncle Charles, that's all. And if he's interested in her, I say fine. But I don't want her using me to get to him."

Sheppy couldn't help smiling. "You mean Mrs. Fletcher *likes* Mr. Montgomery?" she asked, wondering why Miss Montgomery bothered watching soap operas with all that was happening in her real life.

"I don't know. Maybe she just wants a husband."

"But what did that have to do with you? Why was she so mean?"

"To be fair, Fletcher's probably not a bad person. She has a sick mother and she's alone. It's not uncommon for people to take out their unhappiness on others. You know from experience that I'm not innocent of that myself."

It seemed every day Sheppy was finding new reasons to like Miss M.

"But if Mrs. Fletcher's gone, and I'm being fired," Sheppy asked, "who will take care of you?"

"Is that what he said? That you were being fired?"

Sheppy couldn't remember exactly what he'd said now. "I'm not?"

Miss Montgomery shook her head, taking Sheppy's hand. "He *wanted* to fire you when he learned that you had helped me get Turie's letters. He didn't find out on his own, by the way. I told him, *after* I'd read them. Yelled at him, really. I was tired of all the secrets. The lies."

Sheppy just nodded.

"I insisted that you were doing only what I had asked and that you were staying for as long as I wanted you to stay." Miss Montgomery sounded proud that she'd stood up to him.

"Wow! And he agreed?"

"I think I took him a bit by surprise," she said, laughing. Then she turned serious. "And I think it helped that he has been feeling guilty about the accident."

"What do you mean, Miss M? Was it his fault that you broke your leg?"

"He thinks so," Miss M said. "But it was really both of us. We were arguing there at the top of the steps and I somehow stumbled and fell."

Sheppy looked at the stairs and tried to imagine the scene. Then she turned back to Miss M. "But if you said I could stay for as long you want me to, why do I have to leave in two weeks?"

"I'll tell you, but first I don't want you to worry about the money. I've worked it all out with Uncle Charles. We're going to pay you for the rest of the summer. I know your family is depending on your earnings from this job. It wouldn't be right to let you go without compensation."

Sheppy couldn't believe it. Pay her for the whole summer? "But, Miss M, that's not fair."

"You'll be earning your pay, believe me. Although Uncle Charles is taking some time off, I'll be needing you a lot more over the next two weeks, if that's all right with you. After that, I'll expect you to spend at least three hours a day thinking of me. And I hope you'll answer the letters I plan to write."

Sheppy frowned, confused.

Miss Montgomery smiled, her gray eyes shining. She looked beautiful. "I'm taking a trip," she said. "To Marrakesh."

It took a minute for it to sink in. "You mean to Morocco? To see Turie?" Sheppy squealed.

Miss Montgomery nodded. "I sent him a telegram yesterday. He wired back this morning. My doctor thinks two more weeks of using the crutches and I should be strong enough to manage the trip."

Sheppy couldn't stop grinning, but Miss Montgomery wasn't smiling.

"I don't know what's going to happen," she said. "The letters. He's changed. And his telegram. It was nice, but . . . it's been a long time, and I don't know if we can put things right again and start over. Whatever happens, I'm grateful to you, Sheppy. You've given me a chance to put my life back together, put this behind me, if necessary. Uncle Charles and I have a lot to work out, but I think there's hope for us, too. He does care."

Sheppy knew how good Miss Montgomery must be feeling. She'd felt it yesterday, with Ranger, knowing they would sing in the moonlight again. But what about Miss M? Would Sheppy ever see her again?

"When are you coming back?" she asked.

"I don't know. It depends on what I find there. What Turie finds in me. I didn't handle things very well after he was sent back to Morocco. Ended up in a hospital, sick from alcohol."

Sheppy frowned and studied Miss Montgomery's face. She'd only known this woman for a little while, but in that bit of time important things had happened. Things that would always be part of her.

"I've changed, Sheppy."

"It'll work out," Sheppy said, pushing back the darkness that had started to surround them. "It has to. 'Love always wins.' You said so. You have to believe in the possibles."

"The possibles?"

"Something between Papa and me."

Miss Montgomery held Sheppy's hand. "He must have been something, your papa. And what a daughter he's left behind."

Sheppy swelled with pride and sadness. All she could do was smile and remember:

> *Every day I seem to find . . .*
> *Some of you . . . you left behind . . .*

"How about *Words by Heart*? Would you like to finish it today?" Miss Montgomery asked.

"Yes," Sheppy said. "I'm ready now."

Chapter

28

"Hi, Range," Sheppy said getting into the car. She leaned over and kissed his cheek twice.

"Gee!" he said grinning. "Tell me what I did and I'll do it some more."

Sheppy laughed. "You won't believe what's been going on. Miss M . . ." Suddenly she remembered where Ranger had been.

"Hey, how are you?"

Ranger's smile faded. "Okay. Things could be a lot worse, I guess."

Sheppy looked closely at her brother's face for the truth.

"Don't worry, Shep. Really. I feel better than I have in months," he said. "I'm worried about Mama though."

"Me, too."

They rode along in silence. It was good silence this time.

Sheppy loved knowing that when things were right, they could be quiet together and feel close.

"Maybe we could do something for Mama," Sheppy said after a while.

Silence again. Ranger was thinking.

Finally he said, "We haven't been out to the cemetery since the funeral. Maybe we could go visit Papa with her. Think she could handle that? Could you?"

Sheppy's stomach moved slightly, but she said, "I'll go, but how do you think that will help?"

"I'm not sure. Maybe it won't. Maybe it's a bad idea."

He parked the car and they got out. Ranger slipped his arm around her shoulder as they walked to the house.

"We'll talk about it later," he said, holding the door for her. "So, are you keeping me in suspense, or what? Tell me about your Miss M."

"Oh, yes, well . . . wait. Is Mama home?"

"Yeah."

"I want to tell her, too. It's a long story."

. . .

Mama was on the phone when they walked into the kitchen.

"She just came in. I'll put her on." She held the receiver toward Sheppy.

Sheppy mouthed the words, "Who is it?"

Mama just handed her the phone, took Ranger's arm, and pulled him into the living room.

"Hello?"

173

"Hey, Germ."

"Parker?"

"Yeah. It's okay, isn't it? That I called, I mean."

"Sure, but . . . it's long distance and . . ." She thought of the cost but decided not to mention it. "Well, it's a surprise, that's all. You never called me before."

"I never knew you before."

Sheppy felt her face get hot. She was glad he couldn't see her.

"I was going to write, but well, thanks for writing me back. Making me feel okay about telling you stuff. Your father's poem was cool. It made me feel better, so I showed it to my dad. I hope you don't mind."

"I don't mind."

"We talked for about two hours after that. I mean, really talked, about Mom and everything."

"That's great, Parker. So what about your mom?"

"I don't know. Dad says we have to take it a day at a time."

"How's it going with his job?"

"The strike's still on, but he's looking for jobs all over. That's another reason I called. To tell you that Dad found out his old company is hiring again. He's trying to get his old job back."

"You mean you might be coming home?"

"Okay, Aunt Ella. I gotta go, Sheppy. Sorry. I'll write. Hey, I didn't get to ask about you. I'm sorry."

"I'm okay, Parker. I'll write, too."

"Bye."

"Bye."

Sheppy stood in front of the phone for a moment after hanging up. *I never knew you before,* he'd said.

"This *is* getting serious," Ranger said, peeking into the kitchen. Sheppy chased him into the living room, grabbed a pillow from the couch, and whacked him with it.

Mama chuckled and said, "All right you two. Enough." She sat on the couch and patted the seat next to her. "Sit here with me. I want to know what's been going on at the Montgomerys'."

Chapter 29

"Mary Sheppard, you are a prize," Mama said when she'd heard the whole story.

"That's some job." Ranger said. "One month's work and the rest of the summer a paid vacation."

"I *am* a bit uncomfortable with that arrangement," Mama said. "It borders on charity and . . ."

"It's not charity," Ranger cut in. "It's an unusual situation, but Sheppy's earned that money in her own way, Mama. You know she has."

"And, when the two weeks are up, I can help *you* more, Mama, and maybe I can even find another job," Sheppy said. "Then I could make up for Ranger's . . ." She was sorry the second she'd said it.

Sheppy glanced at her brother and caught the look of pain in his eyes. "It's all right, Shep. I lost my job. It's a fact." He paused, then said, "I'm sorry, Mama."

Mama put her arm around him. Sheppy moved closer to her, too, and Mama squeezed them both against her. Silence filled the room. A good silence.

"We should go to the beach this summer," Mama said. "You know how your papa loved the beach. Especially in the springtime. He loved the springtime. Let's see, what was that poem?

> *"I will be with you in May*
> *when there is spring in the air . . ."*

Sheppy looked at Ranger. His eyes filled and he smiled a little. It was the poem Papa had written for Grandfather Lee.

> *"When everything is fresh and new*
> *and beauty everywhere.*
>
> *"We will . . ."*

Mama was thinking, trying to remember.

> *"We will kiss the golden sunrise*
> *and drink the morning dew."*

Sheppy remembered the last lines, and said them with her.

> *"Where buttercups and roses bloom*
> *I shall be with you."*

"You knew, Mama. You knew about the poems."
"Yes, baby, I knew."

"You knew I found them, too, didn't you?"

"Yes."

"But why didn't you ever tell us? Why didn't Papa?"

Mama pressed her cheek against Sheppy's forehead.

"Before . . . he was shy about them. I figured he'd tell you in his own time. Then after . . . well, I'd planned to show them to you at some point, but I haven't been quite up to it."

Before. After. She still couldn't say it. Couldn't say he died.

"When I realized you'd found them downstairs," Mama said, "I decided to let you alone with them for a while." She hugged Sheppy and Ranger tighter. "It's a private thing, finding your way through grief. It will take time for all of us."

Sheppy heard Ranger crying alone in the bathroom. Mama crying alone at night. And Parker's Dad. Parker, too. She saw herself crying silently, reading Papa's poems. Hugging her pillow. Alone. Mama was right. Grief was a private thing.

"Mama, can we go to visit Papa tomorrow?" Sheppy asked.

"I think that's a fine idea, baby."

Dear Papa,

We're coming to visit your grave tomorrow. I wanted to bring something for you, so I'm writing this letter. I miss you, Papa. Everybody does. You probably know about the trouble Ranger's in. Please don't be mad at him.

I still don't know why you had to leave. I don't think I ever will. But thanks for giving us so much. Like your poems. I haven't looked at them all yet, and I don't understand all the ones I've read. Maybe someday I will. And all the other things you taught me. They keep coming back and helping me. Miss M even says I'm one of the good things you left behind. I'm glad that maybe some of you is some of me.

I guess you're not at the graveyard, really. You're in us. Ranger and me. Mama, too.

It's hard without you, Papa. But I think we're going to be okay.

I love you, love you, love you, madly,

Sheppy

About the Author

Vaunda Micheaux Nelson, the youngest of five children, grew up in a small town in southwestern Pennsylvania. She credits her parents with her inspiration to write; for them, she says, "the arts are not just a part of life to be enjoyed, but part of who a person is." As with Sheppy, Ms. Nelson's own father wrote poetry, most of which was unknown to her until after his death. She used some of his poems in *Possibles*.

Ms. Nelson's first book for children, *Always Gramma*, was published in 1988, and her second, *Mayfield Crossing*, in 1993. A children's librarian, she lives in Rio Rancho, New Mexico, with her husband, Drew, also a writer, and their cat, Zipper.